FORSAKE ME NOT

LACYNDA MATHES

This is a work of fiction. Names, characters, places, and incidents are products of the author's imagination or are used fictitiously and are not to be construed as real. Any resemblance to actual events, locations, organizations, or persons, living or dead, is entirely coincidental.

World Castle Publishing, LLC
Pensacola, Florida
Copyright © 2024 Lacynda Mathes
Paperback ISBN: 9798891262188
eBook ISBN: 9798891262195
First Edition World Castle Publishing, LLC, June 3, 2024
http://www.worldcastlepublishing.com
Licensing Notes
Cover: Cover Designs by Karen
Cover-designs-by-karen.com
Editor: Karen Fuller

Dedicated to the memory of Brenda Brownley. You were my mother's friend through thick and thin without judgment. I met up with you by chance as a young woman, out for drinks with a friend, and you caught me smoking. I remember how you feigned shock. I explained that when I drank, I also smoked. You shrugged and said, "So does your mom." It strikes me that this is such a strange thing to remember at this time. There were any myriad of things that I could have thought about upon learning of your tragic passing. I've known you since I was 14. But this is the one that came to my mind as I cried. Because you weren't just my mother's friend, but in that moment, mine as well. Rest in Peace. You'll be missed.

07/21/1957 – 10/21/2023

As always, a special thanks to my family and best friend, Hope Elizabeth Welker, for all her help preparing this manuscript for publication.

PROLOGUE

Mary Cummings stood amid the moving boxes and haphazardly placed furniture. She sighed and opened the box closest to her, marked "living room." She hated unpacking. But she was glad to be home. She looked yearningly out the window at the oak gracing and shading her front yard. She'd been living the last five years in Illinois, and she had missed the trees.

She laughed sadly, thinking of Mike. "We have trees," he'd said at her proclamation.

"You have trees where someone planted them. It's not the same thing. In Virginia, we have houses where we cut the trees down to build them," she'd replied.

He'd been so sick by then, but he'd managed to make her laugh. "So, what you miss is forests, then, not trees," he'd corrected her emotionlessly, almost robotically, without looking her in the eyes, while he'd rocked back and forth in his seat the way he did.

"Eat your soup, Mike," she'd coaxed. "It will make you feel better."

"That's just an old wives' tale, Mary, but I'll try if it makes you happy."

She dug through the box halfheartedly. She could have loved Mike. She surely missed that quirky man. His death was ultimately what brought her back to Virginia. She'd tried staying at the law firm, but seeing his empty office and his father's broken heart on a daily basis had been too much. When her aunt passed and left her the house in Colonial Beach, she'd decided to come home, as he'd told her to do.

Her mother's sister had owned the house but had not actually lived in it. It had been her grandparents' house, where Aunt Berta and her mother had grown up. Meghan had married John Cummings and stayed in Colonial Beach. Aunt Berta had ended up in Florida. When her grandparents had died, they'd left the store and their money to John and Meghan and the house to Berta. Her parents had maintained it. Berta never even came home to attend the funerals. She had her own family and life in Florida. She took ownership but promised the house to Mary. In the end, she kept her promise.

Oddly, one of the last conversations Mary'd had with Mike had been about the house. It had been at Thanksgiving. Being a single woman a long way from home, she'd not had plans for Thanksgiving. Mrs. Davis had asked her to join the family for dinner. When she'd arrived, Mike had been in his apartment over the garage. He'd knocked frantically, if somewhat weakly, on his window and waved for her to come up. She'd donned a mask and gloves and gone into his apartment.

"I'm dying," he'd announced.

She had started to argue, but he'd held up his hand to stop her.

"I'm dying," he had repeated. "I don't get my happy ending. But you can have yours. When your aunt leaves you that house, you have to take it. It's where you want to be."

"I don't know that she will leave me the house," she'd laughed.

"She will," he had smiled.

"How do you know?" she had asked.

"I wrote her will," he'd answered as he held up a file. "My passing gift to you. She's sick, too. Leukemia. Just like me. She said she'd planned to do it anyway. So, when she passes, take the house, Mary. Make yourself happy."

She'd taken the file from him and read the contents. "Wow. Thank you, Mike. You didn't have to do this."

"You're welcome. Can you do something for me? Can you help me give Dan his happy ending?" he'd asked.

"What do you need me to do?" she'd asked.

He had handed her a shoe box. "I wrote it down. It's in the box. I need to sleep now." And just like that, he had been done. She had taken the shoe box, put it in her car, and spent the rest of the day with his family.

She'd seen the shoe box when she was packing. She'd put it in one of the living room boxes. Unfortunately, it wasn't the one she'd opened. She moved on to the next and the next. Finally, she found it in the fifth box she ripped open.

Her phone rang. She pulled it out of her pocket. Noting that it was her cousin, she answered the call. "Theo!"

CHAPTER 1

Camille Camacho stood in front of the mirrors on the pedestal while the seamstress stuck what felt to be the one-millionth pin into the Kelly-green silk. The bridesmaid dress was formfitting, but her form was starting to expand in the middle just a little. "Oh God!" she gagged as she jumped down and ran for the trashcan in the corner. Her breakfast vacated her stomach as Miranda calmly rose from the sofa and rubbed her friend's back.

Deb followed and ran into the bathroom, returning with a cool, wet washcloth for Camille. She gently held it to the back of Camille's neck. "Whoever called it morning sickness obviously paid zero attention to his wife hurling while he was in bed asleep at 10 p.m.," she said sympathetically.

The seamstress smiled coldly. "I'll leave a little more room through the waist."

Miranda snorted. "Bet this is usually the bride's problem, not the Matron of Honor's."

"Certainly was mine," quipped Deb. "But at least Dan was diligent and noticed the 10 p.m. hurling. He didn't stop noticing me for a couple of years, anyway."

"Yeah, I can't wait to marry him! You make him sound quite the catch," Miranda said, batting her eyelashes.

"Oops. I keep forgetting to talk him up," Deb teased.

"You're marrying your bridesmaid's ex-husband?" the

seamstress asked Miranda.

"Yes. Is that unusual?" she asked, stony-faced. The seamstress swallowed hard. "I'm just kidding!" Miranda laughed.

Camille groaned. "Sorry. Well, that was unpleasant. The real shame is that my brand-spanking-new Illinois driver's license has a picture of me five minutes after I threw up. I have to live with that picture for four years. And no offense, Miranda, but green is not my color, at least not on my face." Deb and Miranda were developing quite a rapport. Camille had to admit she was feeling just a tad jealous, but only a tad. Deb was actually quite likeable.

Miranda smiled. "I'm just happy you're here. And I saw your new license. You look beautiful."

The seamstress asked, "If you're feeling better, can we finish your fitting? Or would you prefer I work on the next girl, and come back to you? I'm sorry, but I have another wedding party fitting at 2:00."

Deb smiled. "I'll go. Camille can take a few minutes to recover." Camille smiled, feeling grateful. Deb was alright. And Miranda would never replace her.

The seamstress smiled. "Thanks. And congratulations, by the way.' She patted the pedestal. Deb handed Miranda the cloth and stepped up. "I think the green looks nice on you all," the seamstress winked. "But what's really important is that it makes the bride's hair really pop!"

Deb laughed. "Miranda's hair pops no matter what. But yes, our job is to accentuate her!"

The seamstress finished fitting Deb quickly. Camille, sitting on the sofa, holding the trashcan, waved off, returning to the pedestal. "I guess I'm up," announced Sally Blevins, rising from her seat on the sofa.

Deb retreated into the changing room to take off the

green silk dress and returned in her normal attire: jeans and a tee shirt. Deb was a natural beauty. She looked as good in the jeans as the expensive gown, Camille noted.

Deb picked up her champagne flute as she sat back down beside Miranda. The two women who were partaking clinked their glasses together. The one who couldn't buried her face inside the rim of the trashcan she held. "Here's to your marriage. This time, he's marrying the right girl! And I couldn't be happier for you both," Deb toasted.

"Hear, hear," said Camille, her voice muffled inside the trashcan.

Sally responded, "It's certainly about time. I lost the pool by ten years. So, when was that first kiss, Miranda?"

"Honestly, it was after I got my memory back, and I kissed him. It was after I bought my house. There were lots of near kisses. He just wouldn't pull the trigger," she giggled. "But the real kiss came when he was vulnerable. It was like he needed me to breathe for him. It was… breathtaking…sexy, and sweet at the same time. I felt like I was falling into those green eyes. And then his mouth was over mine, and his hands were…You don't need to know where his hands were. Let's just say they made me tingly. He pulled me in closer, and I felt my legs go limp, but he kept me standing. And the room just sort of melted away. Yeah, it was a good kiss. The best kiss of my life."

"I remember kisses like that. Then I had twins," Camille's voice came from inside the trash can.

"That's…so great. I'd kill for a kiss like that. The best kiss of my life was a long time ago," Deb sighed.

"Do tell," Sally giggled. "Ow!"

"Stop moving," said the seamstress.

Deb laughed. "There's not a lot to tell. I didn't even know his name. And I never told him mine. He was a soldier.

I was 19, and I met him at a Halloween party at NIU. Hardly even a meeting. We hadn't spoken. He was kind of stand-offish, not really interacting. Someone said he'd just gotten back from Afghanistan. My friend I was visiting dared me to kiss him. So, I walked over to where he was standing against a wall and gave him a quick kiss on the lips. It surprised him. He laughed and asked what the hell that was. I giggled and told him my friend dared me. He got this…mischievous, I guess…look and said that I should totally commit to the dare then and not just half-ass it. He put one hand on my back and the other behind the back of my neck. Oh my God, he kissed me…really good. Made my knees wobble. You remember my spider ring? I took it off and gave it to him."

"Wow. What did he look like?" Camille asked, completely enraptured, forgetting to retch.

"It was Halloween. He looked like Zorro. He did have a faint scar running down his neck from under his hair behind his left ear."

"And you?" Miranda laughed.

"Morticia Addams," Deb replied, snorting she laughed so hard.

"Ohhhhhh. That's so romantic. A passionate kiss from an anonymous man…" Sally sighed.

"I'd rather have passionate kisses from the love of my life," Deb replied wistfully. "I just haven't found him yet."

"But I have!" Miranda giggled.

Deb's phone rang. She smiled, and Miranda noticed. She elbowed Deb in the ribs playfully. "Gavin? Ewww, somebody has a crush."

Deb blushed. "He's okay, I guess." Her smile revealed she found him more than okay.

"Well, answer it," came the muffled voice from inside the trashcan. "This old, pregnant woman needs some vicarious romance from the bride and the other bridesmaids."

Sally laughed, getting stuck with a pin as she did. "Ow!"

"Then stop moving," said the seamstress.

"Good luck getting any from me. I haven't had a good date in months. Just a bunch of duds," Sally said sadly, trying not to move.

Deb answered her call. "Hello, Gavin. What's up?" Her smile vanished. She set her flute on the table in front of her. "What?" Her voice was raised and high-pitched.

"What's wrong?" asked Miranda.

Deb sighed heavily. "My mother pulled a Houdini again."

Miranda had told Camille everything. Deb's mother, Kathy, had been committed to a mental health facility for the last five months, ever since she had set her own condo on fire and attempted to run off with her own cousin/brother/lover with money from an armored truck robbery she'd participated in 32 years before. Only her cousin/brother/lover turned out to be more disturbed than she was, and started killing people and stalking Miranda. Unfortunately, she was a bit of an escape artist and kept getting out of where she was supposed to be. She never went far, usually to the cafeteria or common room. And while, technically, Deb was only allowed to visit three times per month and needed to sign up seven days prior, the staff found it beneficial to let her mother see Deb or Deb's sister without the benefit of an actual visit. Just seeing either of her daughters from across a room would calm her enough to convince her to return to her cell peacefully. It was enough to curtail some of those jealous feelings.

"I'm sorry. I have to run," Deb said, rising and gathering her purse. "But I'll see you all tonight at Camille's house."

"Can't wait," came the voice from the trashcan. She

could, but there was no reason to be rude.

"Sure. Hope everything's okay," said Miranda.

"Ow!" said Sally.

"Stop moving," said the seamstress.

CHAPTER 2

Pete Camacho looked out the window of his new office at Moore Robotics. He couldn't believe the view. Lake Michigan spread out at his feet and out beyond the horizon. He knew he owed this change in situation to his wife's friend, or at least to the man she was about to marry. He'd applied for this job every year for the last five. He'd interviewed every year, but this time, he'd mentioned Dan Bradley's name, and here he was, looking over Lake Michigan, from a corner office no less, from the 23rd floor of a Lakeview Drive high rise. His ego felt a little bruised, but…damn…that view was sure something.

He roused from his contemplation as a knock rapped on his office door. "Come in," he called.

"Mr. Camacho?" queried the unfamiliar male voice with a thick Richmond drawl.

"Yes," he replied. "May I help you?" He turned from the window to look at the smiling man at the door.

"I'm willing to bet ya can," said the man as he entered and closed the door behind him.

Pete was confused. He didn't recognize the man. He was certain he hadn't been introduced to him when he started his new job this morning. He motioned for the man to have a seat across from his desk. He sat behind it. "I'm sorry. I don't remember. Have we met?"

"No, Mr. Camacho. Your memory is not failing ya.

We've never met, though I've had the pleasure of meeting your pretty wife. And I'm not here to seek an audience with the new director of engineering. I'm here on a more… domestic matta." The man smiled again, a snakelike smile, his green eyes dead.

"I don't understand," Pete said.

"Please allow me to explain," the man said, setting his briefcase on the desk and opening it. He withdrew a handgun. He pointed it at Pete.

Pete raised his hands. He found it hard to breathe.

The man just continued to smile. He took out a tablet while continuing to point the gun at Pete. He shoved it across the desk. On it was a video feed of his children and Jason Bradley playing at their babysitter's house.

"It's a simple matta, Mr. Camacho. Your children and Jason Bradley are currently in the care of a young lady while your wife, the former Mrs. Bradley, and the future Mrs. Bradley are getting fitted for their wedding attire."

Pete swallowed hard.

The man's smile vanished. "What I really want is for ya to deliver a message. And for ya to understand that I hold all the cards, so ya deliver it exactly how I want ya to."

Pete nodded, sweat forming on his forehead and drenching his new work shirt.

CHAPTER 3

Dan looked at his phone. The incoming call was from Moore Robotics. Pete. He sent it to voicemail. Pete was under the impression he had pulled strings to get him this new job. He hadn't. Whether or not the powers that be at Moore thought Pete might garner them some favor was yet to be determined, but he was willing to allow Pete was smart enough to know what had sparked their interest in him. He hadn't expected the calls to start so soon. He was too busy right now to deal with that nonsense. He turned back to his paperwork. He wanted to be sure he was caught up on everything before his wedding.

The phone buzzed once more. He looked at it again. This time, it was a text from an unknown number. It read, "Take the damn call!" It was just aggressive enough that he paid attention. When Pete called the second time, he answered.

"Hello," he said. As Pete spoke, his face drained of all color. He leaned forward and whispered, "Are you okay, Pete?"

He waved to draw the Sheriff's attention and put the phone on speaker as the Sheriff and Sue Perkins came over.

From the phone, Pete's nervous voice said, "He has a gun on me. But I am fine. He showed me a video of Annalise, Liam, and Jason at the babysitter's. He has told me where Camille, Deb, and Miranda are. His associate is taking Jason.

If I cooperate fully, he will leave Liam and Annalise with the babysitter. He wants 20 minutes before any police arrive, or he will shoot me. He is putting me in a vest with explosives and a cell phone detonator. After those twenty minutes, police may go into the babysitter's house, but if any police stop him leaving this office, he will detonate the explosives. He requires that the bomb squad not interfere until he has left the vicinity, or he will detonate the explosives. No one is to enter or exit this building, or he will detonate the explosives. After an additional twenty minutes, the bomb squad may come in and disarm the device. They will call you from the phone that texted you with further instructions." The phone disconnected.

"Well. Shit," said the Sheriff.

Dan found it hard to breathe. Sue put her hand on his shoulder. "It's okay, Hon." She turned to the Sheriff. "I'll notify the Staties and Chicago PD." The Sheriff nodded at her. She started a stopwatch.

CHAPTER 4

Deb headed north to Elgin. It was a warm spring day. She rode with the window down. She had pulled her hair back in a ponytail so it didn't blow in her eyes. She kept a pair of Oakley's in her minivan. Her Odyssey wasn't nearly as cool as Miranda's Mustang, but with the radio up, she could pretend, especially when Jason didn't occupy his car seat behind her.

Gavin was waiting beside his cruiser as she pulled into the mental health facility's parking lot. He waved as she parked. She smiled, raised her window, and exited the vehicle. She quickly made her way over to him. He smiled and put his hand on the small of her back as they walked together into the visitor's area. She felt a little flutter at his touch.

The guard looked up at her and cleared her and Gavin through. "She's got a real bee in her bonnet today," the woman said.

Deb sighed, "I'm sorry, Janice."

Janice scoffed. "No need to apologize to me, Honey. I don't have to deal with her."

Deb entered the visiting area. Her mother lurched forward, wild-eyed and...panicked. Was that fear she saw in her mother's eyes?

"Jason!" Kathy yelled.

The guards stopped her. "You know the rules, Kathy. You've seen her. Come back to your cell," one said.

Kathy nodded. She made eye contact with Deb and mouthed, "Danger!" Then, she allowed herself to be led out.

Deb looked at Gavin. "What the hell is that about?"

He shrugged, and together, they walked back out through security and back to the parking lot.

They were halfway back to his cruiser when the call came over his radio. Kidnapping in process. Jason Bradley, age three. Orders to stay back, as a bomb was reported in a Chicago office building and would be detonated if police interfered.

Deb fell, stricken, to her knees and screamed a primordial cry. Gavin pulled her to her feet and into his arms. He stood there in the parking lot, holding her up and to him. The sun slipped behind a cloud, casting a shadow over them. She screamed. He held her. Finally, her scream stopped, and her tears started. She was conscious of the world again, though. She wrapped her arms around his neck and cried onto his shirt again, just like she had five months ago when she had accepted her nightmare of her father's murder as a memory.

As she regained her composure, he led her to his cruiser. He opened the passenger side door and sat her in the seat. "Give me your keys, Deb. I'm not letting you drive."

She handed them over emotionlessly, dazed. He called for another trooper to come get her car. They sat in silence while they waited. He reached over and held her hand. She squeezed his in response to his gesture.

In a few minutes' time, a trooper rapped on Gavin's window. Gavin lowered it. "Hey, Tim. Thanks for coming. I didn't think she was in any condition to drive."

Tim nodded. "Yeah. I understand. I have two kids of my own. The youngest is three. We'll get him back, Mrs. Bradley."

"It's Ms. I'm divorced," she responded under her breath.

Tim took the keys Gavin handed to him and walked to Deb's Odyssey.

CHAPTER 5

Due to the use of explosives, the FBI claimed jurisdiction. Dan found himself relegated to being the victim and the victim only. Agent Mathews told him only what he needed to know. The Sheriff and the state police were more forthcoming, but they were pushed back to support only. Agent Mathews ran the show.

Special Agent Thomas Mathews was a year short of retiring. He was experienced and professional. His only concern was getting the child back. He didn't give a good damn who Dan Bradley was. Trust-fund baby, he assumed. Worse, trust fund baby who wanted to play cops and robbers. He wanted the man nowhere near his operation. He preferred the friend. The State Cop. He at least had to work for a living.

Both the fiancé and ex-wife were good looking. Pretty women loved money.

Once the twenty minutes expired, Agent Mathews gave the order to enter the house. It was a standard suburban home, just like the two on either side of it. Inside, they found the teenager, hired for the day to watch the kids, in tears. The Camacho twins were sitting in her lap, also crying. She held onto those kids like a tigress, though. She screamed like a banshee and kicked when the officers tried to pry the kids away from her. A female officer finally talked the girl down, convincing her they were the authorities. Poor kid.

The Camacho kids' mother was at the scene. The officers released her children to her. She nearly smothered those kids. It would be a few more minutes before the Chicago PD bomb squad would move in and work on getting the vest off her husband. She was hysterical. Understandable, but hardly helpful.

Agent Mathews growled and approached Dan Bradley. This dipshit was going to be difficult to manage. All that money plus a deputy's badge could not be a good combination.

"Mr. Bradley. I'm Special Agent Thomas Mathews. If you cooperate fully, we'll get your son back. If you decide you know better than me, you'll screw this up. Do you understand me?"

"Special Agent Mathews, I am not an idiot. If you feel the need to be condescending to me for whatever reason, I don't really care. Just get my son back. Okay?" Dan replied.

The older man was unconvinced, but at least the deputy was cooperating at the moment.

"Tell me about the call."

"Wouldn't it be more beneficial for you to hear the call?"

The agent huffed. "And how do you expect me to do that? Do you have a time machine, Mr. Bradley?"

"No, sir, but I do have a recording app on my phone. I recorded the call," Dan replied. "Again, I'm not an idiot."

The fiancé gave Agent Mathews the evil eye. The Sheriff winked at him. He sighed again. "My apologies. Please." He motioned for Dan to play the recording.

Having heard the call and gleaning no information from it that had not already been established, the agent looked at his watch. "We need to set up a command center and wait for further instructions."

"My parents' house is there," said the fiancé, pointing to the biggest house in the neighborhood, a block up on the left of them.

Agent Mathews nodded. The rich sure had it good. But the security gate would be beneficial. It would keep the press back, at least.

CHAPTER 6

Miranda ushered Deb, Camille, and the kids into the kitchen, where Connie was peeling tomatoes. She'd let Dan deal with that arrogant FBI agent. "Wine?" she asked the ladies.

Connie pointed to the wine cooler. "Just let me have the Chianti for the sauce." She continued peeling.

"Mom, I believe you are a stress cooker," Miranda said, opening the cooler and examining the options. "Merlot okay?" she asked.

"Yes. Anything," replied Deb, emotionlessly. Her face was blank.

"Mommy, you're squeezing my fingers," said Annalise.

"Oh, I'm sorry, Baby," Camille said, letting go of the twins' hands for the first time since she'd gotten them back. She kneeled and hugged them each. "I'm so happy to have you back with me."

Connie pointed to the breakfast nook. "You two want to help me make spaghetti sauce? You can crush tomatoes for me. Auntie Randi and her twin, Mike, used to help me all the time."

"Yep, cheap child labor," Miranda quipped, grateful to her mother for distracting the kids. She poured three glasses of the Merlot, emptying the bottle. She handed one to her mother and then gave Deb a glass. She downed her own in three large gulps. "Ahhhhh. Nothing like drinking Merlot like it's whiskey."

Miranda grabbed a second bottle and took it to the family room. She sat on the sofa, looking out the bay window.

No sooner had the FBI set up their equipment in the family room than Pete, having been released from the explosive vest without incident, arrived at the gate. After a slight skirmish with the police not wanting to let him in, Camille ran down to the gate. Miranda watched through the window as he pushed past the police, and they fell into each other's arms. Camille started kissing his face everywhere.

Agent Mathews interrupted their reunion from the portico. "Mr. Camacho? A word, please."

Camille slipped her arm around his waist. He draped his around her shoulders, and they held each other up as they walked to the door, the gate closing behind them.

"Are the kids alright?" he asked as they entered the house.

She nodded. "Scared, but okay. They took Jason, Pete."

"I know. I'm so sorry. I...I didn't have a choice! There were 532 people in that building! I feel so useless," he responded.

Dan greeted him from his seat on the third stair. "Don't. Pete, you did great. You got everybody out safely. You're one of the bravest men I've ever met!" Tears ran down his cheeks, and he buried his face in his hand as he sobbed.

Camille stepped forward and wrapped her arms around his neck. "I wish there was something we could do."

"Well, Mr. Camacho saw one of the kidnappers. He can sit in here with our sketch artist and give us a description," announced Agent Mathews, somewhat impatiently.

"Yes, of course. No problem," he said. He and Camille followed the agent into the family room.

Deb emerged from the butler's pantry from the back

of the foyer. Miranda turned to see Deb sit on the step beside Dan. She touched his knee and laid her head on his shoulder. "I feel wholly disconnected from everything," she announced. "Isn't that weird? Have I lost my mind?"

Dan kissed the top of her head. "No."

"Are you sure?" she asked him.

"I'm sure. I feel the same way."

Miranda felt numb. But a weird numb. She felt like she was having some kind of premonition of coming evil.

"Why do you say the man was from Virginia?" the agent's voice bellowed from behind her.

"His accent," Pete's voice replied. "Richmond, or nearby, I'd say. Plus, he said he knew Camille."

"And you'd know a Richmond accent from any other southern accent?" huffed the agent.

"Well...yeah," Pete replied. "I'm from Richmond."

"And you didn't know him? Even though he knew your wife? And you come from the same town?"

"No, sir. There's two hundred thousand people in Richmond. Do you know two hundred thousand people?"

The agent huffed again.

Dan's cell rang. "Agent Mathews!" he called.

The agent waved him into the room. Dan answered the call on speaker.

"H... hello," he said, clearing his throat.

"Hello, Deputy Bradley. Hello Miranda," said the voice.

Miranda went pale. There it was. The coming evil.

"Hello, Kris," she squeaked out as she found her voice. Kris Bowen. The man who had raped her in college. She felt the need to vomit. She dove for the trashcan behind the bar just to her left.

She evacuated the contents of her stomach, wiped her

mouth, and stood up. The sketch artist held up the sketch based on Pete's description. There he was, staring at her from the page like he'd done that morning when she had come to: Kris Bowen, evil incarnate, as far as she could tell.

"Kris, don't hurt him!" she pleaded. Tears rolled down her face as she sat on the floor.

"You mean he deserves more than what our baby deserved? You killed our baby, Miranda," Kris's voice came over the speaker, evil, hissing, snakelike.

Dan stared at his distraught fiancé as she curled in on herself, hugging her knees to her chest. She sobbed openly.

"You son of a..." Dan yelled, slamming his fist onto the coffee table.

"There, there, Deputy. Watch your language. You want your kid back? Do as I say..."

CHAPTER 7

Kris disconnected before they could trace the call. He demanded $1,000,000 in small bills be delivered by Miranda to a grave located in the West Batavia Cemetery at 900 S Batavia Ave at 8:30 in the evening. The days were getting long, but as it was still spring and not yet summer, that would be just after dark. She was to put the money in her old college backpack. He conceded she would not come alone, but he insisted that it be Pete who accompanied her. They were to be dropped off at the gate and walk inside. They were to find the grave of William Arthur Tinsdale, born April 12, 1959, passed May 8, 1962. They were to place the backpack on the gravestone and leave the way they came in. They were to walk, not run. Once the money was retrieved, the child would be dropped off at the gate.

As Miranda walked stoically beside Pete through the open gates and amid the tombstones, as the sun set, she couldn't help but wonder what Kris really wanted because, as sure as the graves around her, she was certain it wasn't money. Money had never been a motivation for him. He had it in spades. Old money. Tobacco money. It was meaningless paper to him. A million dollars was nothing.

She had never wanted to go out with him. He was arrogant, snivelly, slimy. And it wasn't the money that made him that way. His brother was none of those. Camille was dating Kris's twin, Sean Bowen, at the time. It was before she met Pete. Sean was easygoing, funny, kind, and humble. She had learned that he died seven years ago. A car accident. She wouldn't put it past Kris to have tampered with the car… or rather have paid someone to tamper with the car. He was above getting his hands dirty. Literally, that is. He had OCD.

She had first met him in her dorm room freshman year. Sean had come to pick up Camille for a family dinner. Kris, being the arrogant ass he was, had burst into the room like he was God himself.

"Whatta hail are ya doin'? Let's go!" Emphasis on the "o."

"Camille idn't ready yet, Kris. We're comin,'" Sean had replied.

Then Kris had turned to her. He had actually licked his lips. "Well, hello, pretty lady. And who might ya be?"

"That's Miranda Davis, Camille's roommate. Miranda, this is my brotha, Kris," Sean had said, making the introduction.

"Will ya be joinin' us for supper, Miss Davis?" Kris had said, coming uncomfortably close to her. The question seemed suggestive coming out of his mouth.

"Um. No. Thank you. I have a test tomorrow." She hadn't, really.

"Well, Christ, ya sound like a Yankee, Gerl." He had laughed.

"Chicago," Miranda had replied.

He had licked his lips again and leaned in even closer. She had leaned back to escape his proximity.

"A pretty gurl like ya doesn't need to wurry about hir grades," he had whispered. His breath had been hot. It didn't smell. He was too vain to allow that, but it had been unpleasant nonetheless.

Her thoughts were interrupted by Pete's declaring,

"Here it is. William Arthur Tinsdale. Age three. Beloved child of...Kris and Annalise." He was silent for a moment. "He's one crazy son-of-a-bitch."

Miranda took off the backpack. She placed it on top of the tombstone as she had been instructed to do. She was crying. But she held her head up. She wouldn't give him the satisfaction of seeing her break. And she knew he was watching. She could feel his eyes on her.

She slipped her arm through Pete's, and they walked back out the way they had gone in.

CHAPTER 8

Gavin looked at the twin sisters, sitting side by side in the afternoon sun. Sharon was sitting on the bench. Sara, after years of working the trapeze and high wire, had just had her hip replaced and was still in a wheelchair most of the day, though her doctors reported she was doing very well.

"Hello, Ladies," he said, announcing his presence.

"Sergeant Mahoney! Hello," Sara greeted him. "How's my granddaughter?"

"Not great at the moment, Mrs. Zamphir."

She blushed. He did it on purpose. He knew she'd renounced it decades ago when she learned that her husband had cheated on her and fathered her nephew, Victor. She'd forgiven Sharon, but not Bart. Gavin wanted to see her reaction.

"Her son, Jason, your great-grandson, has been kidnapped. The thing is, Kathy seemed to know it was about to happen. She tried to warn Deb. We asked her about it. She told us the guy had visited her and made threats. But when we asked why she believed him, she said I should ask you."

"Me?" Sara was genuinely surprised. "Well, if I know anything, I'll certainly tell you!"

"She said I should ask you about 'Monica.'"

"Monica? I don't understand. What could Monica have to do with Jason? That was 65 years ago."

"What was?"

Sara blushed. "I had a baby sixty-five years ago. I was seventeen at the time. I was scared. I went to Booth Memorial in Minnesota. He was born April 16, 1959. I gave my son up for adoption. I never even saw him. He was Bart's son, too. I only ever loved Bart. My mother made me go. But when I was released, Bart was there. I chose him. And I never looked back," she smiled. "He never blamed me."

"Monica?" Gavin interrupted, sitting beside Sharon, who scooted to allow him room between them.

"Wasn't she your roommate?" Sharon offered, helping to bring Sara back to the question at hand.

"Monica. Oh, yes. She was. She was only fifteen years old. I was scared and confused, but she was beyond terrified. Apparently, she had had an affair with a married man. Plus, she came from a wealthy family. She was really messed up. She was madly in love with the father. And she believed he loved her, but he was really too old for her. I really blame him. He should have known better. She had a boy, too. The day after my son was born. Anyway, her adoption was prearranged by her father, so the kid went to some wealthy family. My son's adoption was arranged by the hospital. I really hope he found a good home. I've worried about him for sixty-five years. Of course, Francie came along a year later. I bet they'd have been close."

She drifted into the past again.

Sharon reached over and patted her sister's arm. "I'm sure they would have been."

"I should have forgiven Bart, you know," she said, tears in her eyes.

"It's never too late, Dear Heart," her sister crooned. "He'll know."

Sara burst into laughter. "Yes, I believe he will know.

And maybe he'll even forgive me."

Her mind cleared again, and she looked at Gavin, perplexed. "What could Monica possibly have to do with poor little Jason's being kidnapped?" She wrung her hands in obvious worry and concern.

Gavin shrugged. "I don't know, Sara. But I'll try to figure it out. Kathy isn't always lucid. She still has delusions. Maybe it's nothing. But I'll check it out. Do you know Monica's last name?"

"No. We never used last names," she said, tears filling her eyes.

CHAPTER 9

The money sat there untouched for an hour and a half before a frightened elderly woman in a Caravan minivan pulled up to the agents waiting in an FBI van at the cemetery gate. She rolled down her window and yelled for help.

An agent approached the van. Jason sat quietly in the back, sucking on a Dum Dum. The woman tearfully explained a man was holding her wiener, ironically named Oscar, at gunpoint. He had instructed her to bring the child, whom he had brought with him into her house when he had pushed his way in 30 minutes ago, to the gates of this cemetery, where she was told the FBI would take custody of the child.

Agent Mathews himself ran into the graveyard. The money was still on the tombstone. As Miranda had suspected, this was never about money.

Agent Mathews questioned the old woman. Her name was Beverly Mattox. She had lived in Batavia her entire life. She had never been to Virginia. She didn't know anybody in Virginia. She'd never seen the man before. And would someone please go save Oscar? Agent Mathews condescendingly dismissed her story. She was involved. She had to be. He grabbed her roughly and cuffed her, shoving her into the back of a squad car, declaring she'd answer his questions "downtown."

That's when the Sheriff arrived with Dan and Deb. He

had brought them to reunite them with their son. He looked at the woman, who was now crying hysterically. He walked over and tapped the agent on his shoulder.

"What can I do for you, Sheriff?" Agent Mathews huffed.

"Well, you can tell me why you have Alderman Mattox's mother in the back of that squad car?"

"Alderman…"

" Alderman Jared Mattox. Yes. He's been on Batavia city council for twenty years. Ward 5. That's his mother, Beverly," explained the Sheriff, pointing at the woman.

As the agent's face fell and he shook his head in disbelief, the Sheriff smiled. "Well, at least it isn't the mayor's mom, Special Agent Mathews. You'd look like a real dipshit then. Foley! Go check on Bev Mattox's dog!"

From back behind the police line, the young deputy yelled, "Yes, Sir." He promptly turned and jogged to his cruiser.

CHAPTER 10

"I assure you, we don't take kindly to people wasting our time, Mr. Bradley! I do not care to spend my time investigating a prank pulled by an old boyfriend! The kid doesn't even seem scared! Says you and his 'uncle' were coming to get him!" Agent Mathews yelled, poking Dan in the chest.

Dan clenched. "One. He is not an 'old boyfriend.' He's a rapist she went out with one time. Two. The explosives he put on Pete were real. So, I wouldn't classify this as a prank! Three. Jason's three. I don't know what uncle he thinks was coming to get him, but he knows I was. I'm his father, and I always tell him I'll come get him no matter what. It sounds like he was coping to me!"

Agent Mathews huffed and walked through the French doors and into the family room. Dan turned and walked over to where Miranda sat on the stairs. He sat down beside her. She laid her head on his shoulder. He wrapped his arm around her waist and pulled her close.

"Why didn't you tell me you got pregnant?" he whispered.

She shrugged, tears welling in her eyes. "I was afraid of what you'd think."

Dan looked at her, puzzled.

She smiled. "I didn't have an abortion, Dan. No matter what Kris Bowen may think. I went to the clinic. Mike took me. But all the way there, we talked. It wasn't what I wanted. He told me he would support whatever decision I made. I got into the gown at the clinic. And I...I couldn't. I decided to have the baby and give it up for adoption. I got dressed. I walked out. And Mike brought me home. The next morning, he contacted Dad's law partner, Martin Feldman, for me. He had handled several adoptions. He agreed to see me. But before I could go...I lost the baby."

"What about any of that do you think would make me think less of you?"

She shrugged again, a tear rolling down her cheek. Her lip trembled. "The part where I thought less of me: that I considered abortion, that I changed my mind, that I was going to give it up, that I couldn't carry it to term...that I was pregnant, to begin with? Or that he raped me, and I didn't have the courage to do anything about it?"

"Jesus," he whispered. He kissed her forehead and wiped the tear from her cheek with his thumb. "Okay. You told me about the rape years ago. So that wasn't it. I knew you didn't report it. I understood. You were eighteen, Honey. Eighteen. You have more courage than any woman I know. I was adopted. My mother was adopted. I would have supported that decision. But miscarriages are beyond your control, Love. There is nothing you've just said that would give me a second's pause."

She sniffed and closed her eyes. "Rape confuses everything, Dan. It isn't rational. I know that. But I was still afraid of how you'd react, of what you'd think of me, irrational as it sounds. And, as you can see, Kris's evil. I guess he scares me, too. Talking about him...fills me with utter dread."

He sat, holding her quietly. She cried some more. He stroked her hair. "I love you, Miranda. I will always love you. I'm not going anywhere."

"Promise?" she whispered.

"That's kind of the whole point of this wedding thing, isn't it? But yes, I promise." He kissed her forehead again. "Gavin went to walk Buddy for me. Should I just get him to bring him here tonight?"

She shook her head. "No. I want to go home. To our home. Okay?"

"Okay," he replied, pulling her close and kissing her lips. "Mmmmm. Salty."

She smiled and wiped her eyes with the back of her hand.

CHAPTER 11

Having walked Buddy and checked the townhouse on Wind Energy Pass where Dan and Miranda lived and finding nothing amiss, Gavin brought Deb and Jason home. Katelynn, Deb's sister, was staying in Rock Island over the summer, having gotten a much-prized internship at John Deere in Moline. Dan didn't want them alone. Neither did Gavin, for that matter. He had feelings he wasn't ready to admit, mainly because he didn't think she was ready. He followed them in, carrying his overnight bag.

Deb flipped on the light and let out a startled yelp. "Ahhhhh! Jesus! Uncle Bob! You've really got to stop letting yourself in! What are you doing sitting in the dark?"

Bob had moved back to the area after his sister had been committed. He was taking on the responsibility of taking care of their elderly mother and wanted to be closer to see his sister more regularly. Frank, the oldest of the siblings, had arthritis, and the cold winters were too much for him. He decided to leave the day-to-day stuff to Bob and stayed in California.

Bob smiled and rose from his seat in the armchair. "I was just contemplating, Dear Heart. Just contemplating. Hello, Jason. I'm so glad you are home! I've missed you." Jason ran to his great-uncle and jumped into his arms. Uncle Bob gave the boy an "airplane" around the living room. Jason didn't seem to notice that he had been in any danger. He was just happy to see Uncle Bob, who was fast becoming his favorite, non-parental relative. Bob "landed" Jason by tossing him gently onto the sofa. He feigned breathlessness. He was in as good shape as Gavin, and Gavin was in superb shape. "Oh, dear. You wear out this old man!" he exclaimed. "go play in your room for a bit, please. I want to talk to your mommy and Sergeant Mahoney."

Jason giggled. "He's just Gabin, Uncle Bob. You don't have to call him Sardant Mahoney."

"He's right," Gavin assured the older man, shaking his hand.

Bob grinned. "I'd be pleased. Please, just call me Bob, as well." He sat back down in the armchair as Jason ran off to his room. "I've searched the house. It's safe," he added.

Deb sighed in relief and sat on the sofa. Gavin sat beside her. Her hand brushed his leg, and he felt butterflies.

"What upset Kata today, Gavin?" Bob asked, reverting to using his sister's childhood nickname.

"I completely forgot Mom in all the confusion," Deb said, looking at Gavin. "I hadn't thought of it since it had happened. I've been too preoccupied with being terrified. But apparently, you have."

He shrugged, embarrassed under her scrutiny. "Apparently, Kris Bowen visited her yesterday. She'd never met him. She had no idea who he was, but somehow, he got approval to visit. He put the fear of God into her. Or the Devil. He seemed to take pleasure in telling her what he planned to do to Jason. None of which he did. He's demented."

The older man nodded. "Yes. Apparently. I see you have brought an overnight bag. Good. I'll sleep easier."

Gavin smiled. "Yes, Sir. I'll stay as long as I need to."

Bob grinned. "My brother, you call 'Sir.' Not me."

Gavin grinned. Bob was no fool. He knew more than he let on. "I was wrong, you know. When I said Kata wouldn't like you. She speaks highly of you, Gavin. I have come to accept we did more harm than good by protecting her the way we did," Uncle Bob said. "I hope Dan and Miranda are well. It's been a hell of a day." He looked down the hall. "Just the same, I think I'll stay here tonight, Debbie. For my own peace of mind."

She nodded. "Sure, Uncle Bob."

He stood and walked back to Jason's room, where Gavin knew he'd already set up his sleeping bag. Deb had told him she'd found Bob sleeping in there more than once since he'd moved back.

Her uncle was a widower, Gavin had learned. His wife had passed away 15 years ago from breast cancer. He had three sons, all of whom were married. He had grandchildren. But his sons had all moved away in the last year. One had gone to Boston, one to Seattle, and the third to Santa Fe. He suddenly found himself alone. It was obvious he had given his heart to Jason.

Gavin reached to grab his overnight bag. He was going to take it to the den. He'd stayed in there more than once. Deb grabbed his hand. "Leave it for a minute, please," she asked. Her crystal blue eyes pleading with him to stay.

"I'm not going anywhere, DeBella. I'll sit here as long as you want," he replied. He called her by her given name, and she sighed softly, almost smiling in response.

She lay her head on his shoulder. "It's been a terrible day. I just…need some human contact."

He put his arm over her shoulders and pulled her close. It was pure torture.

She lifted her head to look at him. "Did you get a haircut?" she asked, playing with his hair.

He laughed. It was such an absurd question, given the events of the day. "Yeah, I got a haircut."

She laughed, too. She took his face into her hands and turned his face away from her. "Look, you can see your neck behind your ears," she giggled. Then she fell silent. Oh crap, he thought, the scar...She'll think I'm some kind of crazy stalker. But she didn't say anything.

CHAPTER 12

She and Gavin sat together for a few minutes. She picked up the TV remote and flipped through the channels in silence. Her heart was racing. It was him. She knew it. Her heart had been telling her it was him from the beginning.

"Anything you wanna watch?" she asked. Her mouth went dry.

"Whatever you like," he said, clearing his throat and staring straight ahead.

She found "The Big Bang Theory" playing on a channel. They watched for a few minutes. The Sheldon character claimed to have an eidetic memory. Gavin snorted. "He's describing superior autobiographical memory, not eidetic," he scoffed.

She looked at Gavin and turned off the television.

"What?" he asked. Was he nervous? He sounded nervous. He was never nervous. Cool. Aloof. Emotionless. Never nervous.

Screw it, she thought, giving into the urge. It was him. She leaned in and kissed him, wrapping her arms around his neck and climbing onto his lap, straddling him.

"Oh," he replied to his own question. He put his hand on her back and then the other behind her neck and pulled her in for another kiss. She'd hoped he would be amenable to her advance, but as the kiss continued, she felt her body surrender to his control. She wasn't kissing him. He was kissing her. And she hadn't been kissed like that since... She kissed his throat and nibbled his left ear. She ran her finger over the silvery-white scar that ran behind it.

She pulled away, breathing heavily, leaned back, and pulled her shirt over her head, throwing it behind her. He ran the back of his hand gently down the inside of her still raised arm to her hip. She moaned and leaned in, brushing her lips against his neck. "I'm not a scared teenage girl anymore," she whispered.

He whispered back, "You were never scared, Morticia."

"No, I guess not, Don Diego. I was just...inexperienced. Were you ever going to tell me?"

"Eventually."

"Cool," she said and kissed him again, unbuttoning his shirt.

CHAPTER 13

Dan slid into bed beside Miranda. She rolled to face him. She smiled at him, but he read fear in her eyes.

She leaned on her elbow and picked at the blanket with her fingers.

"Kris Bowen is dangerous, Dan. I told myself I would never let him make me a victim. I told myself I'd never be afraid of him. But I am afraid of him."

Dan nodded. "I am, too. He wants to take what I love more than life itself. He took Jason. He wants to take you. He has clearly shown he is someone to be feared, even if nobody was hurt…YET. But I promise I will die before I let him hurt you."

"Losing you would hurt me," she replied.

"Miranda," he whispered, closing his eyes, "I'm never leaving you. Never."

"I told you what happened. The GHB in my drink. The waking up in that cabin out in the woods. Not knowing where I was or how I got there. Knowing only that I hurt… where I shouldn't hurt. I don't remember the actual rape." She cried as she spoke.

Dan reached out and took her hand. "I want to kill him," he hissed.

"Why is he doing this? Why now?"

"I don't know, Baby. I honestly don't know."

"He didn't do any of the things he told Kathy he was going to do to Jason. He said he was going to cut off his fingers and toes. He said he was going to slash his face and peel back his skin. He said he was going to break his thumbs and knees. And when he couldn't stand the pain, and only when he couldn't stand the pain, he'd shoot him in the stomach and let him die slowly. Do you think that is what he means to do to me?" she asked, trembling.

"I don't know, but I won't let it happen. I promise."

She laid back on her pillow and looked at the ceiling. "I know. You always make me feel safe." She intertwined her fingers with his.

"How did Mike react to all this?" he asked, thinking about his best friend. Mike had been Miranda's twin, but they had been as different as night and day. Miranda was fiery, passionate, and reactionary. Mike, who had passed away a year and a half ago, had been contemplative, stoic, controlled. He had rarely shown emotion. But, still, he had loved deeply. His family. His friend. His treacherous bitch of a girlfriend, who had cheated on him and cleaned out their accounts and apartment when she left. She was gone now, too. A victim of the same murderous conspiracy as Mike.

"He reacted the same way he did when Wendy Welker ratted me out for having a flask at prom," she laughed. He loved hearing it. It was normal. It meant she was okay.

He laughed, too, at the memory. Mike had had a crush on Wendy in middle school. She was still a pretty girl. Unfortunately, she was a "mean girl." Mike had a type. Maybe he identified bitchiness as a compensation for a lack of social awareness. Or, more likely, he just didn't even notice bitchiness at all. What he noticed was his sister's reaction to situations. He didn't understand her reactions, but he recognized them.

Miranda had gone to prom with Wendy's ex-boyfriend, Griffin Jonas, a quarterback. At his request, she had snuck a flask in her purse. Wendy had somehow got wind of it and had told Mr. Bonaventure, the vice principal and chaperone. He had confiscated the flask and kicked Miranda out. Additionally, she had been suspended for a week.

Mike had seen his sister escorted out of the prom. He had seen the humiliation and disappointment on her face. He had seen Wendy laughing at Miranda. He hadn't known what had happened or what any of those emotions were, for that matter. He had just known they weren't the emotions he was supposed to be witnessing. He stood up and walked across the dance floor. As the song ended, he asked loudly and somewhat robotically, "Wendy, did you hurt Miranda?"

Wendy had just laughed in his face, much as she had when he'd asked her to a middle school dance. "Go sit down, Retard."

That was the word that always got a reaction from Mike. He had been smarter than any of them. He processed things differently. He was not retarded. He hated that word. Unfortunately for Wendy, she had hurled it at him while standing next to the refreshments, most notably a cake proclaiming in cursive writing the prom's theme of "Teenage Dream." He had turned to the table, picked up two pieces of the cake, and smashed them into her boobs. Then, just as emotionlessly, he had said, "Oops."

He had not been suspended. Mr. Bonaventure had spoken with Sam for an hour and decided after that he would let Mike's parents handle the disciplinary action. Sam had taken Mike out for ice cream, but he was under no circumstances to order sprinkles. In typical Mike fashion, he told his father he didn't like sprinkles. That was the end of it. Miranda rightly served her suspension and was grounded for a month.

"He smashed cake in his boobs?" Dan snorted.

"No. Tacos. And he dumped them in his lap," she laughed. "I called Mike right after… It was Friday morning. He was on the first plane to Richmond that afternoon. Camille picked him up while I was in the infirmary. Kris was having that weekly dinner with his family at a Mexican restaurant in Richmond. Camille hadn't broken up with Sean yet, so she knew where they were. He and Camille drove straight there from the airport. Camille told me that he walked in, walked straight over, and, in his emotionless way, told Kris to stay away from me. Kris asked what he planned to do about it…I can imagine how condescending he must have been. Mike dumped the plate in his lap and said…"

"Oops," Dan finished for her.

"Yeah. Then he dropped Mr. Park's card on top of the tacos and said, 'If you go near her again, I'll let our attorney handle it.' Cool as a cucumber. Because he was always cool as a cucumber," she snorted. "Anyway, Kris's father grabbed Kris by the collar and made him promise Mike he'd leave me alone. Right there in the restaurant."

Dan was quiet for a minute.

"What are you thinking?" she asked.

"I'm thinking: where is his father now?"

CHAPTER 14

Gavin wrapped his arms around Deb's waist, snuggling his face into the curve of her neck, kissing the back of her shoulder. She purred in response, turning herself inside his embrace to face him. She smiled and kissed him, entangling her limbs with his once again. They lost themselves in the moment, not noticing the small person standing at the foot of the bed.

"Mommy?"

"Oh crap!" Gavin exclaimed, pushing himself away from Deb. He wasn't often surprised by people walking up on him.

She gently put a hand on his shoulder, blushing. "It's okay," she mouthed. He'd have to trust her on that. This was a completely new scenario to him. He'd never...with a mom.

"What is it, Honey?" she asked, pulling the covers up over her more tightly.

"I had a bad dream," Jason said, tearfully.

"Ahhhhh. I'm sorry, Baby," she said, patting the bed beside her. Jason climbed up next to her. She made sure she was covered with her left hand and slung her right arm around his shoulders, hugging him to her. She kissed the top of his head. "I know all about bad dreams. Do you want to tell me about it?"

He shook his head. "Can I have a glass of wadar?" he asked meekly.

"Sure, Honey," she crooned, reaching back, smacking Gavin, and holding her hand open for him to hand her something. He looked around and spied his own tee shirt on the floor by the bed. He reached down, grabbed it, and placed it in her hand. She grabbed it from him and pushed Jason away gently. "Let's go to the kitchen." As the boy turned away to stand, she quickly slipped into the tee shirt and hopped out of bed, throwing the covers back over Gavin in one swift movement. It was honestly impressive.

As they reached the door, the boy stopped and looked up at his mother, "Mommy, are you gonna marwie Gabin like Daddy is gonna marwie Nana?"

"Uhhhhhh," she stammered.

Gavin grinned. "Yeah, are you?" he teased.

She snorted. "Not at the moment, Jason. We like each other a lot. Romantically. Do you know what that means?"

He nodded, "That you kiss and stuff."

"Exactly. But we aren't ready to get married. Okay?"

"Otay," he replied.

Gavin laughed as she took the boy out. He ran his hand over the sheets where she had just been lying, feeling the warmth she'd left. "Oh my God," he chuckled, laying back into the pillow and closing his eyes.

******

She led Jason out of the room and got him water. Uncle Bob was sleeping soundly in his sleeping bag on the floor when she tucked Jason back into his bed.

"Mommy, I hope you do marwie Gabin. He's Daddy's bes friend. Daddy likes him a lot better than Mawk," he said as she stood to leave. It was the first time he had mentioned Mark in months since Mark had been murdered in December. He turned over and closed his eyes. The sleep of the innocent, she thought.

She returned to her bedroom to find Gavin sitting on the end of the bed. He had dressed, minus his tee shirt. She kicked the door closed behind her, pulled off his shirt, and threw it at him. "Where are you going?" she asked with a grin. "We aren't done kissing and stuff."

She stepped closer. He grabbed her wrists and somehow twisted and flipped her so that she ended up on her back with her hands above her head. He brushed her hair away from her face and lowered himself on top of her, kissing her again. Moving to her neck, he nibbled just below her ear, making her instinctively arch her back.

Through bated breaths, she said, "Damn, you're a good kisser."

"Just a good kisser?" he asked, moving his hand down her neck, around the inside swell of her breast, and slowly down to her belly and over her navel. Then he did something that turned her brain to mush: he whispered in her ear, "*Fuiste hecha para ser besada por mí.*"

"Oh no. It's all very, very good," she said, letting out a moan of pleasure as his hand moved lower.

CHAPTER 15

The next morning, Gavin drove Deb and Jason to the townhouse on Wind Energy Pass. Dan and Buddy, Dan's exuberant cocker spaniel puppy, greeted them at the door. Dan let them in, swooping the puppy up into his arms and kissing it on the nose.

Miranda was sitting at the dining room table, her plate of bacon and eggs still untouched in front of her. "Hey. Are you guys hungry?" she asked, rising from her seat, revealing her mother's influence as a hostess.

"No, we had beckfas at Mommy's house," Jason said, reaching for the puppy. Dan smiled and put the dog in his son's arms. Buddy furiously licked the child's face. He giggled. Can I go pay wit Buddy outside?" he asked.

"No, Honey. I want you to stay inside with us." Deb replied.

"Otay. Poor Uncle Bob is gonna be lonely out dare all by hisself." He pointed out the window overlooking the back yard.

They turned to look. "Ah, Christ!" exclaimed Dan, startled to see Bob in his backyard. "Damn, Deb, you know Bob freaks me out."

"I didn't know he was coming here, Dan. He comes and goes as he pleases. You know that," she snickered.

Miranda giggled. "As long as Uncle Bob is with you

and Buddy, you can play outside, Jason." She knew that Dan found the man creepy, with his pale skin, dark hair, unusually young features, and ability to appear and disappear at will, but she found him charming and amusing. He was a bit of a criminal, no doubt. But he would protect Jason at all costs.

Jason beamed, looking to his father for approval. Dan begrudgingly nodded. Jason took his father's hand and led him toward the basement stairs and the back door leading to the enclosed backyard. "Come say hi to Uncle Bob, Daddy. He said he wanted to tawk to you."

"Really? When did he say that?"

"Last night, after Mommy put me back to bed when I had a bad dream when she was kissing Gabin."

Gavin's back stiffened, and he blushed. Deb snorted and bit her thumbnail.

"Mommy was kissing Gavin, huh?" Dan asked, following Jason and wagging his index finger at his friend.

"Yas. In her bedoom. See put on his tee swirt to go get me wadar," Jason continued.

"Oh, Dear Lord!" Gavin cringed. "It keeps getting worse." He stomped his foot on the floor. "Open, damnit. Swallow me whole."

Miranda swallowed her laughter and sat back in her seat, staring at her plate until Dan and Jason had left the room. Once they heard the back door open, she looked up at Deb, "Good for you!" she quipped.

"Sure was," Deb replied, sitting in the chair next to her, laughing. "A few times." She picked up a piece of bacon off Miranda's plate and broke it, popping half in her mouth smugly.

"Oh geez!" Gavin exclaimed, embarrassed.

"Don't you know girlfriends tell each other everything, Gavin?" Miranda smiled. She was enjoying his discomfort. It was nice to see him have a human reaction. She'd never seen him embarrassed. And noticing that, she realized she'd never seen any range of emotion, really. He smiled. He laughed. But only just enough. It seemed like he was never overwhelmed by emotion.

"Yeah. Just never seen it in person. Even my sister closed the door on me first," he answered, walking around the table to sit opposite Deb.

Miranda winked. "Have you met me? I'm told I'm rather blunt."

Deb reached across the table and grabbed his hand. "And I'm her fiancé's ex-wife. What can I say? He has a type."

They both cracked up.

"You two can be really creepy together. You know that?" Gavin asked, giving them a wary look.

Miranda heard his words, but what she saw was a guy who always stifled his feelings. Deb deserved someone who didn't do that. She wasn't sure Gavin Mahoney could or should give into that kind of reckless abandon.

******

Dan reemerged from the basement to find Gavin sitting with his head in his hand as the women laughed. "Go easy on him, Ladies."

He motioned for Gavin to come with him. Gavin, his blush just starting to fade, let go of Deb's hand and followed Dan back to the basement.

"What did Bob have to say?" Gavin asked, his voice breaking.

Dan laughed. "It's cool, Man. I gave you the greenlight a while ago." He smacked Gavin on the shoulder. "As for Jason, he's a little kid. He pops up unexpectedly at the worst possible moment. He isn't going to be traumatized by walking in on you. At least I hope not, or I'm screwed."

Gavin nodded. "Oh crap!" he suddenly exclaimed. "I still haven't asked her out!"

"I think she'll say yes," Dan guffawed. Then he pointed out the door at Bob, who stood statue-like, watching Jason play. "He told me Frank went to Virginia this morning to visit their cousin's daughter, aged 24. Her name is Theodosia Bowen. Maiden name, Zamphir. Seems her husband recently passed away, and she's concerned her stepson is trying to cut her out of her inheritance. She's also worried he may have killed the old man. You have any leave you can take?"

"Sure," Gavin replied. "What about them?" He motioned to the ceiling.

"Well, you couldn't have picked a more opportune moment to become a couple," Dan winked. "I'm thinking we take Jason to see Uncle Brandon in Sterling. Your dad will be nearby, and he'll be safe there. Besides, Bob won't let him out of his sight. And the four of us go on a pre-wedding couple's trip to visit my stepmother." Dan's adoptive father had remarried four years before he had passed away to a teacher, and the two of them had moved to a small town in Virginia. She still lived there.

Dan had set up a home office in the basement, having tired of working at the kitchen table. He made a few calls and arranged for his grandmother's private jet, which he had moved to the Kane County airport since inheriting in November, to be ready at 7 p.m. Gavin called his cousin, who, in a strange twist of fate, had been revealed to be Deb's half-brother. Brandon and his wife, Melissa, agreed to meet them at the Dekalb rest stop off I 88 and take Jason for the week. They were warned that Uncle Bob would likely be lurking but that he was not a danger, just creepy. They both called into their respective law enforcement agencies, taking leave before heading back upstairs and revealing the plan to Deb and Miranda.

CHAPTER 16

Meanwhile, Miranda leaned in closer, asking for the juicy details. Deb wasn't bashful, not about sex, not about much anymore. The shy girl in high school had grown into an outgoing, friendly, confident woman.

"What changed in you, Deb?" Miranda asked after Deb did indeed share the intimate details, which included the consumption of a bottle of tequila.

"What do you mean?" Deb laughed.

"Well, in high school, you were…different," Miranda said, sipping her coffee.

"Shy and creepy?" Deb laughed.

"You had a Wednesday Addams vibe, yes," Miranda agreed.

"You really do say whatever you think, huh? Refreshing." Then Deb sighed. "I don't know, really. I wanted to go to Notre Dame. But Mom couldn't afford the tuition. I had to get rid of the goth-girl crap and get a job."

"Yeah, but that's just trappings, the exterior. You… you've lit up like a lightbulb since then."

"Yeah, well, sitting there watching the world pass you by and never saying what you think doesn't get you what you want in life."

"Oh, I know. But I mean, something had to have made you realize this and put it into action."

"You don't really want to know. It's silly. And ultimately, I was wrong. I won't come out well in retrospect," Deb protested.

"Deb, I promise I won't judge you. I adore you!"

"Yeah, well, it has to do with Mike."

"Okay," Miranda said.

"He came into Macy's with Vanessa while I was working."

"And you couldn't believe someone like him had a girlfriend? You weren't alone. I don't think he could believe it!" Miranda laughed.

Deb blushed. "I feel like a judgmental ass for thinking it."

"Well, good. You should. And so do I. Because it was honestly what I thought, too. Now that we've established that we are both human beings who can be judgmental and also feel bad about it, go on."

"Anyway, he kissed her."

"He did? In public?" Miranda brightened.

"He did. The funny thing was he asked her if she was his girlfriend first. He didn't even rock when he asked. I thought it was the cutest thing I'd ever witnessed. I overcame my fear and went over to him and asked how he got the courage."

"What did he say?" Miranda beamed.

"That the only way to know what someone else is thinking is to ask. The only way to live is to do what scares you. Then he looked really sad. He said bad things can happen if you let your anxiety stop you from doing what you should do yourself. Then he said I should be bold. He knew I could be because I just had been by talking to him."

"Bad things? What did he mean by that?"

"No idea. But he had genuine sadness over it. Real emotion."

"When was this?"

"Um…fall…August or September? First year after high school."

"He felt guilty?"

"Um…maybe. I just thought sad. But guilt could be right. Anyway, I decided to be braver. Turns out it was really just a choice."

Miranda frowned.

"Hey, I'm sorry. I told you it would be hurtful to hear," Deb said, reaching out and taking Miranda's hand.

"Oh, no. Honey, it isn't about you. You're fine. It's about Mike. He felt guilty. That kills me. I think it had to do with Kris Bowen." Then she forced a smile and changed the subject. "So… Gavin Mahoney?"

"Mmmmm. Yeah," Deb sighed.

"I'm glad. But be careful, Deb. He's a little…intense."

"You don't like him?" Deb asked, sounding concerned.

"Oh, no. I like him. I do. Promise. I just worry he doesn't share a lot about himself."

Deb smiled. "Yeah, Dan's an open book. Gavin has something…I don't know, a dark shadow hanging over him. I get that. I'll be careful, Randi. But he really does care about me. I'm sure of that." Miranda nodded in response.

CHAPTER 17

If Miranda had learned anything in the last six months, it was money moved mountains. Planning a wedding? Throw money at it, and it gets done. Want to go to Virginia on a moment's notice, with a bag full of cash and fully loaded weapons for a week just a month before that wedding? Throw money at it. Miranda was convinced the biggest issue they'd encounter would be convincing Sam Davis to stay in Chicago. She was certain he wouldn't want to let his daughter out of his sight. But he surprised her by not arguing at all. He even volunteered to take Buddy for them. In the end, he watched the plane take off from outside the airport without any objections.

A limo was waiting for them on the tarmac when they landed at Byrd Field. As soon as they were situated in the limo, Deb called Brandon to check on Jason and then Katelynn. Miranda called her parents and Camille, who felt a little left out, but Miranda explained that it wasn't a pleasure trip and that Camille needed to be with Pete and her own kids, not chasing after a madman. She promised that the next trip would include them. A little over an hour later, they were at the VRBO house Dan had rented that morning.

It was dark by the time they arrived, but the house was on the Potomac, in a housing development called Westmoreland Shores, on a small point where the mouth of

Monroe Bay emptied into the Potomac, opposite to the town of Colonial Beach. The sound of the river, six miles wide at this point, lapping at the shore, was soothing and rhythmic.

The house itself was a modern structure, blocky in its architecture, 2 stories built on top of the ground level garage, which opened on both the front and river facing sides to allow the river egress in a storm surge. An industrial-grade steel staircase led up the side of the house to the front door over the garage. There was an elevator tucked in between concrete encased support beams inside the garage that they used, two at a time, to enter instead to avoid using the staircase in the dark.

Dan turned on the lights upon exiting the elevator. The house, though small, was amazing. The kitchen and living room were open, and there was an enclosed sunroom and balcony along the entire riverside of the house. There was a full Jack and Jill bath and two large bedrooms on the main floor. There was a circular staircase leading to the top floor, where the master suite was located. The décor was tasteful, beachy, and comfortable.

"Wow. Nice." Miranda commented.

"Not bad at all. Can't wait to see the view. Wish this really was a vacation."

The elevator returned to the garage for Gavin and Deb.

Miranda ran her hand across the large granite-topped island. "Mom would love this kitchen."

Dan hugged her from behind, kissing her cheek. "Maybe I'll buy this place."

The elevator doors opened. Deb stepped off. "Where's the outside light switch? Gavin went out to check around the house after the limo left. I said I'd switch the light on so he could come up the stairs."

"Probably by the door," Miranda suggested, pointing

to the entrance. Deb dropped her bag and dragged Gavin's off the elevator, and walked over, finding the switch. She opened the door, and Gavin came in. He smiled as he entered.

"The house is nearly as big as the lot, but from what I can see, it is a sweet location. Looks like a yacht club or something right there," he said, pointing.

"There is," Dan laughed. "It actually burned down about twenty years ago, so it's fairly new."

"So, how are we going to get around without a vehicle?" Deb asked.

Dan grinned. "It's nice having money. I bought two Escalades this morning. They're delivering them tomorrow morning."

"What is it with you and Escalades, anyway?" asked Gavin, taking a seat on the sofa and turning on the television with the remote that was sitting on a side table. He opened his bag and took out his service weapon, setting it on the coffee table.

"They make me feel like Elvis on steroids," Dan winked.

"Ah, yes. The Elvis thing," Gavin smirked.

"What Elvis thing?" Dan asked.

Miranda laughed. Gavin was right. Dan had an Elvis thing. The slight pompadour, the sideburns. Mike's influence, no doubt. Mike had adored Elvis Presley movies.

Deb picked the bedroom closest to the living area, insisting that Dan and Miranda take the master suite "since Mr. Moneybags is paying for it."

"Sold!" exclaimed Dan with a laugh. "Speaking of which, here," he added, tossing a sizable stack of the cash from Miranda's backpack to Gavin, "pay for anything you need or want with this. I don't want this trip costing either of you anything."

Miranda shook her head. He was actually having fun. Never mind he was here looking for a maniac. He grabbed his and Miranda's bags and bounded up the stairs with them.

"Wow. He's like a kid in a candy store," commented Miranda, following behind him. "Well, *that's* a good view!" she added, admiring his rear as he walked up the stairs.

Deb looked at Gavin. He kicked off his shoes and leaned back. "I'm not walking up those stairs. If you wanted a show, you should have come outside with me. But if you'd like to head up, I'd be happy to watch."

She laughed and sat in his lap instead.

"That works, too," he whispered with a smile. She leaned in and kissed him.

Then, there was a knock at the door.

"Dan, you expecting anyone?" Gavin called.

"Nope," Dan answered, coming quickly back down the stairs, his own service weapon in his shoulder holster. Miranda stood on the landing, looking down. She thought she might vomit. She nervously came back down the steps.

Gavin moved Deb off his lap and picked up his, holstering it at his waist. Deb and Miranda stood together at the corner, peering around at the door.

Dan flipped on the outside. His brow knit in a quizzical expression. The light revealed a Westmoreland County Deputy standing on the platform at the top of the stairs, just on the other side of the door. Miranda relaxed and moved to Dan's side. He slipped his arm around her waist.

Dan opened the door and asked, "May I help you, Deputy?"

The deputy peered inside, eyeing Gavin, who stood behind Dan and Miranda. He ignored Dan and his weapon but was obviously keenly aware of Gavin's. "Had a report of a prowler outside."

Dan's green eyes flashed in anger. "Really? A prowler? Well, my friend, Illinois State Police Master Sergeant Gavin Mahoney, was just outside, and he didn't see anyone. Did you, Gav?"

"Not a soul," Gavin replied. "Do you have a description? So we can be on the lookout." He showed his badge.

The deputy blushed. "Um. Latino male, tall, fit. Obviously, a mistake."

"Obviously," Gavin replied. "Did the caller happen to mention the half-Irish part?" Miranda snorted. Gavin could be quite snarky.

"No, sir. I'm sorry. I just answered the call is all." The poor deputy was obviously mortified.

Dan laughed suddenly. "It's okay, Deputy. We're both officers of the law. I'm a Deputy myself in Kane County, Illinois. We know the call comes in; you check it out. Our issue isn't with you."

The deputy sighed in relief. "Thanks. I appreciate it. I'm Manny Jaurez, by the way," he laughed.

Gavin burst out laughing. "You're Mexican by way of…Germany, I'm guessing, from that blond mane?"

"Scottish and German, yes. My dad is Mexican, but I look like my mama."

"And I look like mine!" Gavin guffawed.

"So, you folks on vacation?" he asked, returning to his purpose for being at the door.

"We are," Dan replied. "I rented the house for the week on VRBO. Need to see the confirmation?"

"If you don't mind too much," Manny admitted. "I kind of understand why the neighbors are wary. We have had a woman go missing in the last day or so. Her house was tossed, and she's nowhere to be found."

Dan pulled his phone out of his back pocket and pulled

up the app for the deputy, who recorded the information and left.

Dan and Miranda went back up the spiral staircase. Gavin sat back on the sofa beside Deb. She leaned against him as he slipped his arm around her shoulders and propped his feet up on the table. Miranda looked down from the landing and noticed a transformation.

"Dan," she whispered, "look."

He looked down at his friend and ex-wife. "Yeah, so? Gavin's been into her for a while."

Miranda rolled her eyes. "Everybody knows that. I'm talking about...their faces."

Dan looked again. "Okay?" he said, questioning.

"It's like they...found home...the second he draped his arm around her." She turned to look at her fiancé. "I like Gavin. I do. But he's...kind of intense sometimes. He's hard to read. You really can't tell what he's thinking. You...you're an open book," she laughed.

He took her hand, leading her away from the railing. "It's true. I don't know exactly why he's so intense to use your word. I do know he served in Afghanistan. And I do know he's way smarter than he lets on, way smarter than me." Miranda scoffed. He laughed. "Thanks, Babe. But it's true. I looked him up. He's got Ph.Ds behind his name. Plural. And he speaks several languages. Not just English and Spanish. He like minored in Russian. I mean, who minors in Russian? Talk to him for a minute. You'll see. He'll start...teaching...on some obscure subject...like he did with that mullo thing. You remember? He knew exactly what it was, and he explained it. Then, when questioned about how he knows these things, he'll brush it off that he read it somewhere, or someone told him about it. I talked to Sara Walters. She didn't know squat about mullo. He's a lot like Mike in that way...being way smarter than anyone else. The difference is Mike let everyone know it. He tries to hide it."

Miranda hugged him. "I don't care what you say. Maybe he's more educated, but he's not smarter." She kissed him. He smiled, and she saw the same transformation come over his face she'd noticed on their friends. "Oh my God, Dan. They aren't just into each other! They love each other!"

"Yeah, I know."

"Do they?"

He laughed. "I think they have an inkling."

God, his laughter still sounded like a choir of angels. She kissed him again, this time more focused on him.

CHAPTER 18

Miranda pulled away from Dan and slipped into a robe. "I'm thirsty," she announced.

"Do you want anything?"

"Mmmmm. No, thank you," he said with a smile. "Just hurry back."

She made her way down the circular staircase and over to the fridge, which just happened to be situated between the door to the two bedrooms on this floor. She opened the refrigerator door, the little light illuminating the darkness of the house. She reached for a bottle of water.

She dropped it when Deb screamed. Through the closed door, she heard Deb scream in terror and then yell, "Mark! No! Gavin! Gavin!" It made her jump, and it drew Dan from the bed they were sharing and halfway down the stairs.

"DeBella! Shhhh! I'm right here! I'm here!" came Gavin's voice through the door. "Look! I'm okay!"

Then Deb, sounding scared but calmer, replied. "Oh. Okay. I'm sorry. Just a nightmare."

"It's okay. Are you alright?"

"Yeah. I'm going to get some air."

Miranda stood there with the fridge door open, staring in horror as the bedroom door opened and Deb emerged. Miranda felt like a deer caught in headlights as Deb saw her.

"Oh, I'm sorry, Randi. I just have nightmares since… I'm okay. Hope I didn't scare you guys too badly. I'm just going to get some air."

She turned, waved to Dan, and headed out onto the balcony overlooking the river.

Miranda started to step forward, but Gavin emerged and headed after her with a nod to both Miranda and Dan. So, she just grabbed her water and headed back upstairs. She went to the picture window that looked down on the balcony. She didn't want to eavesdrop, but she wanted to be sure Deb was okay, so she looked down on Deb as Gavin came up behind her. He encircled her waist with his arms. She leaned back against him. He kissed the side of her head.

"You want to talk about it?" Miranda heard him ask gently.

Deb shook her head no. "The same as last night," she said.

"Do you want to stop…go back to just friends?" he asked.

Deb laughed and turned to face him, throwing her arms around his neck, standing on tippy toes to kiss him on the mouth. "God, no! It isn't because we're together. I've been having that dream since you stayed in my den that night."

"Oh," he replied. She knew it. Reserved. Aloof. No passion.

But then he leaned down to kiss Deb, pulling her closer until there was no space between them. Miranda saw the two of them kiss. It was incredibly intimate, and she felt embarrassed to be eavesdropping on them. She turned to walk away when she heard Gavin's husky voice moan… "Hey, Morticia."

She turned back to the window as Deb replied, "Hey, Don Diego. Wanna make out?"

He laughed and said suggestively, "I dare ya."

Miranda's mouth dropped open.

Dan grabbed her hand and pulled her away. Her mouth still agape, she pointed at the window. "What?" he asked, laughing at her.

"Did Deb ever tell you about her best kiss ever?" she whispered excitedly, thinking that isn't the kind of thing you tell your partner if it wasn't shared with him.

Dan wrinkled his nose. "Are you asking me about kissing Deb?"

"No, I'm asking if she *told* you about *her* best kiss ever."

"Meaning I'm not the one who gave it to her? Then no. I'm guessing she told you." Dan laughed. It didn't matter anymore. He wasn't threatened by the news.

Miranda sat on the bed and patted it for Dan to sit. She leaned forward in a conspiratorial pose. He laughed and sat. Miranda related the story of the Halloween party kiss.

When she got to the part about the guy having just returned from Afghanistan, he raised an eyebrow. "And you think it was Gavin?" he asked.

"Well, he just called her Morticia!"

"Have you met her uncles?" he chuckled.

Frustrated with him, she countered, "She called him Don Diego! That's Zorro, right?"

Dan stood, walked over to the window, and opened it. "Hey, Gav!" he called.

"Yeah?" Gavin answered from below.

"Did you, dressed as Zorro, kiss Debbie, dressed as Morticia Addams, about 11 years ago at a Halloween Party?"

"Yeah," Gavin replied without any hesitation or embarrassment in his voice.

"That kiss is apparently the stuff of legends," Dan chuckled.

"Really?"

"I know, right? I'm going to kiss the hell out of Miranda now to dispel any doubts about my abilities."

"Sounds like a plan," Gavin called out. Deb giggled.

Dan shut the window and flopped on the bed, pulling Miranda down and kissing her.

"You're kind of a jerk," she laughed.

"Yeah," he laughed back. "But who cares if they kissed 11 years ago? What's the big deal?"

"It's a big deal, Dan. For her, it's a big deal!"

He sat up. "You're worried about her?" It was as if he hadn't realized this before. Of course, she was worried about her!

"He's really intense and hard to read," she said.

"No. He's not. He's hurt and careful. Just like her."

CHAPTER 19

Morning came brightly. Literally, the sun shone in through the windows and reflected off the Potomac, warming the air quickly. The group rose to what felt like a midsummer day, though it was only late May.

Miranda, as her mother would do, raided the kitchen, which their host had fully stocked for them. She rummaged through the kitchen, finding pans, utensils, and knives. She chopped onions, peppers, mushrooms, and potatoes. She found eggs, ham, and mozzarella in the refrigerator. She fried the potatoes and veggies in a cast iron skillet before adding in the eggs, meat, and cheese, finishing it off as a frittata. She put on a pot of coffee, the smell of which called to the others like a siren song. They ate as if they were famished.

The Escalades were delivered promptly at 9 a.m., one red, one silver, both showroom models. Dan signed the paperwork and paid in cash. He registered them both in his and Ava Bradley's name at her residence a few miles away from where they were staying. Miranda saw him smile as he did it. He was playing Elvis, knowing he'd sign them over to his stepmother as soon as they were done.

At approximately 9:30, Frank Walters appeared at the door, along with his cousin's daughter, Theodosia Bowen.

Frank looked exactly as he had for the last twenty years or so: clean-shaven, even his skull, and pale, seemingly more so under the brightness of the day. He was slow coming up the stairs, using a cane due to his arthritic knees and back. The arthritis was the only indication of age. He, like his brother, had an amazingly youthful appearance and fit physique.

Theodosia was exactly as Miranda expected: a trophy wife, tall, thin but curvy, with big hair, big boobs, expensive clothes, and makeup. She was stunning in her own way but unremarkable, especially in contrast to the creepiness of her companion, which stood out like a sore thumb. Dan shuddered as he let Frank into the house. Frank grinned slyly, noticing it.

"Hi, Uncle Frank!" called Deb from the balcony. "Want some coffee? Don't worry, Miranda made it."

"What does that mean?" asked Theodosia, obviously confused.

"That I'm not interested in her for her culinary skills," muttered Gavin.

Frank nodded. "Your cousin is not gifted with the skills required to prepare a good cup of coffee or anything else in the kitchen, but Miss Davis is. Deb, my dear, this is my cousin Nicu's daughter. Theo, this is Debbie. Her mother is my sister, Kata," he said, hobbling out onto the balcony.

Deb rose, squinting at the sun and reaching out to shake the girl's hand. The girl ignored it. "Who's Nicu, again?" Deb asked.

Frank replied, "Your grandfather had two brothers, Ilya and Maxim. Nicu is Ilya's youngest son, ten years younger than your mother."

"It's nice to meet you, but I really don't understand how she can help me, Francie," said Theo.

"Not her, Dear; her gentleman friend and ex-husband," Frank replied, motioning to Dan and Gavin, who sat at a table drinking their coffee in the sunroom behind them. They both waved casually. "They're police officers. And they're particularly interested in bringing your stepson to justice."

"Justice?" she asked.

He motioned again, this time to Miranda. "She's Miranda Davis, dear. She's engaged to Deputy Bradley. Deb's ex."

"Miranda Davis? The girl?" Her voice was thick with incredulity.

"Well, I used to be a girl," Miranda replied with a huff.

"I'm sorry. I just expected someone more my age from the way Kris talked."

"Kris's older than me!" Miranda exclaimed.

"Is he? Oh, well. I guess I don't see him that way, being his Daddy's wife and all." She walked back into the sunroom, leaving Deb standing with her hand extended. She sat down across from Dan and Gavin at the table.

She shimmied in her seat and smiled, leaning forward to reveal her cleavage. She tossed her hair and smiled again. "Well, I don't care who finds him, you or that nice Agent Mathews I talked to last night. I think he killed his Daddy and means to kill me. That's why Francie came out, to watch over me." She leaned closer and whispered, "He's really creepy, but it kinda makes me feel safer to have him around. I don't think Kris can hurt him."

"Not without a wooden stake," Dan whispered back.

"To paraphrase Adam Sandler, 'Who wouldn't be hurt by a wooden stake being driven into their chest?'" whispered Frank, appearing suddenly behind Dan.

"Ah. Geez, Frank!" exclaimed Dan, jumping, "I hate it when you guys do that."

Frank snickered. "Yes, I know. Jason has gotten quite good at it, Bob tells me."

"Frank! Are you two teaching him that crap? He walked in on me and Deb the other night! Scared the crap out of me!" scolded Gavin. Frank scrutinized Gavin again. The reaction he was looking for never registered on Gavin's face. The familiarity was strictly the result of his relationship with Frank's niece. That was good.

Frank answered with his sly smile and by raising one eyebrow.

"I don't get it," said Theo.

The three of them turned to look at the girl, mouths slightly agape. Deb sat back down, "Jesus Christ," she mumbled.

Miranda stepped out onto the balcony and sat slowly next to Deb, stifling her laugh. "Oh, my God," she mouthed to Deb.

"Anyway," the girl continued, "I have evidence that he had someone tamper with his brother's car. Wally had it in his wall safe. It's a video the guy took, showing him asking him to cut the brakes and payin' him to do it. Before he died two weeks ago, he showed Kris the video and told him he was cutting him outta the will, leaving it all to me. He showed him the will and everything. I saw it. Then, when Wally up and died for no reason that night, the will turned up missin' the next mornin.' But Wally'd changed the combination on the safe, so I still had the tape. I gave that nice agent the original. But I made copies cuz I'm not dumb." She pulled a flash drive from her purse and handed it to Dan. "I still got copies," she added, in a tone implying some kind of warning.

"Why would that matter to us?" Gavin asked.

"I'm not sure," she replied, "But I wanted ya to know so you don't try to pull something."

"Okay," he said, still looking befuddled.

"Well, I don't know you, do I?"

"Um. Okay," Dan placated. "We won't try anything,"

She smiled as if she had won a prize. Miranda didn't

quite know what to make of her. She was brash and rude…
and a little stupid, but her intentions seemed pure enough.

"Like I said, Wally just up and died for no reason that
night. He went to bed and never got up. He'd just had a full
work up, too. The doctor said he was as healthy as a horse. I
think Kris poisoned him or something. They're doing a full
autopsy, at my request, cuz I'm his wife, but I think that rat
may try to kill me before we get the results, like he did his
brother 7 years ago and his daddy two weeks ago. He started
hitting on me. You think Francie is creepy? Kris is way worse.
He started tellin' me what he did to that Yankee redhead.
That's what he called her. Showed me the video. Told me
he'd do worse to me cuz I'm a bigger…whore. He called me
a whore. Anyway, that video was bad," she said, tears filling
her eyes. For the first time, she seemed sympathetic. "I'm
sure sorry you had to go through that, Ma'am." She turned to
speak to Miranda.

Miranda nodded. Her throat was tight. *He still had the
video?* She felt panicky all of a sudden. She had no memory of
the actual attack. He could have just had sex with her. It would
still have been rape because she was unable to consent, but he
didn't do that. He'd taunted her, belittled her. He'd choked
her. He'd held a bowie knife to her throat and her private
areas. He'd bound her. He'd done unspeakable things, being
careful to leave no marks. But terrorizing her. And because
he knew she'd never remember it, he'd made a video of it and
forced her to watch it when she'd awakened the next day. Out
in a cabin, in the woods, where she didn't know where she
was or how to escape. It had turned out to be in King George
County, about twenty minutes away from Mary Washington
University. He'd dropped her off after he'd made her watch
it five times. Dan often wondered at her bravery in the face
of danger. She knew the source. She'd already lived through

hell.

Dan's head shot up. "Video?" He rose and walked to where Miranda sat beside Deb. He kneeled in front of her, gently taking her hands into his. "Miranda, you never told me about a video..." His voice was tight, cracking.

"I never told anyone. Not Mike. Not Camille. Not even my therapist. Once you know, Dan, you can't unknow." She looked at him, imploring him to love her still in her expression. He squeezed her hands lovingly.

"I want to know everything, my love. There is nothing that will scare me away," he assured her.

She sighed. "You know how...disturbed... I was that I still couldn't remember October 27th after I regained my memory?"

He nodded.

"It was because of what he did to me. Because I can't remember any of it. Not to this day. I only remember the video. Which he forced me to watch while I was naked, afraid, hurt, and tied to a bed, and gagged. Over and over. It wasn't as simple as date rape, which would have been bad enough. He was a coward. He wanted to rape me. But he didn't want the inconvenience of my fighting back. So, he drugged me. Knowing I'd never remember, he recorded the attack." She proceeded to reveal all the horrific details. He kneeled silently throughout, tears welling in his eyes.

He sobbed as she explained the brutality the video had revealed. "So, when you couldn't remember the 27th, you thought maybe?"

She nodded and looked at the river. Her voice caught in her throat as she continued. "There's more. I think Caleb Guthrie had seen the video."

"What? Why?"

She turned back to him, searching his face, seeing only

concern for her, only love in his eyes.

"On the video. At one point, Kris removed the gag. I said I was thirsty. He asked me what I wanted to drink." She paused, not wanting to continue. He squeezed her hand again to encourage her. "I asked for milk," she spat out.

Dan's eyes widened. "No. No." He shook his head.

She sighed. "He drank it himself, standing over me. Then he dumped the rest of the carton on me. Caleb Guthrie did the same thing. It's probably what triggered the amnesia to begin with." A tear ran down her face.

Dan threw his arms around her waist, pulling her to him. "Oh my God! Miranda, why didn't you tell me? Miranda! Miranda!" She collapsed into his embrace, hugging him tightly. He smothered her face in kisses as he repeated her name.

Deb, sitting there beside her, wiped her own tears and pulled her knees to her chest, hugging them. "Damn," she whispered.

Theo, appearing at least cognitive to the headiness of the moment, cleared her throat. "Well, I don't know what you're talking about with Caleb Guthrie, but Wally had a chauffeur named Cain Guthrie a couple of years ago. He was like twenty years old. In Louisiana. We lived in New Orleans for like six months." She unwittingly confirmed Miranda's suspicion.

Dan pulled back suddenly, grasping Miranda's shoulders. "Have I ever scared you? Demanded something that scared you?"

"No, my love. You've only ever made me feel complete, loved, and cherished." She smiled at him and kissed him gently on his lips.

His green eyes, which could flash in anger, reflected only concern. "I wish I had known, understood why Caleb freaked you out so much."

"No one knew. Not even me until I remembered what happened on the 27th."

"Did Caleb...do anything else?"

She shook her head. "No."

Frank sat down in the chair Dan had vacated beside Gavin. "Kris Bowen is a coward. No doubt. But he's a dangerous coward who acts on his dark fantasies."

Gavin nodded. "Yes, Frank. I believe you are right."

Theo turned to Gavin. "Well, he's sure pissed she got an abortion after he raped her, so she should be aware."

"What?" asked Gavin, startled.

"I didn't!" Miranda exclaimed. "I went to the clinic... over Thanksgiving break...but I couldn't...I miscarried!"

"Well, he knows you went to that clinic. And he thinks you went through with it," Theo added.

"What difference would it make if you had? He's still the monster here," Deb spat angrily.

Dan pulled the folded sketch artist's rendition out of his back pocket and walked back to the table. He tossed it down in the center of the table. "Kris Bowen," he said.

Frank nodded slowly but held his tongue. He looked at Gavin again, this time thinking he caught a glimmer of recognition crossing the officer's face, but then Gavin looked puzzled and shook his head, and the glimmer vanished to the point Frank doubted he had seen it.

CHAPTER 20

Miranda allowed Theo wasn't a genius by any stretch of the imagination, but she meant well enough, in her own greedy way. She gave them the location of the cabin in King George, a location Miranda had never known. He'd blindfolded her again before dumping her in his car, left her tied at the hands and feet until he'd gotten onto Route 3 when he'd stopped, cut her loose, and removed the blindfold, warning her to keep quiet. She'd obeyed.

Theo said she wanted to get back to Richmond, that the country life in the Northern Neck was unappealing to a girl from Miami, where Ilya, her grandfather, had settled when he was with Ringling Brothers. So, Frank took her away, giving Dan's shoulder a squeeze as he helped him down the stairs and into the driver's seat of the Miata Theo had insisted they drive. Miranda followed behind them.

"Thank you, Frank. I really appreciate this. Take care of her. She's alright," Dan smiled.

"You're welcome, dear boy. I told you: we like your bride and, God knows, we love your boy. We're not so very scary, really."

Dan laughed. "No. In the scheme of things, I guess not."

Frank closed the door and drove off with the top down. Dan wrapped his arm around Miranda, and they waved goodbye from the driveway.

A neighbor, working in her flower bed at the front of her house, watched the Miata drive away with an obvious intensity. Dan smiled and waved at her before taking out his phone and sending a message to the VRBO host. Then they climbed the stairs and went back to the balcony.

"I promise you, Miranda. You'll never have to worry about that son of a bitch again. Never," he said as they walked.

She smiled and kissed him. "Don't do anything you'll regret, Danny. I already know that."

"I won't regret a thing," he swore.

"I'm not sure about that girl," Gavin proclaimed. "I only believed maybe a quarter of what she said."

Dan nodded. "I understand, but I think she means well. I trust Frank even if he creeps me out."

"Frank…isn't…He doesn't figure into my issues with Theo. He believes her. I don't."

"Noted. But I believe enough…Is that good enough?" Dan asked.

Gavin looked conflicted, but he said no more and just nodded.

Miranda felt her stomach lurch, and she ran to the sink. She barely made it before her breakfast vacated her stomach.

Deb jumped up and came to Miranda's aid. She turned on the faucet and grabbed a clean cloth from the drawer. She pulled Miranda's hair back and held it, rubbing her back while she vomited. Then when Miranda started to cry, Deb gave her a gentle squeeze. She wet the cloth and wiped Miranda's face. "Is it all up?" she asked. Miranda nodded.

Deb helped her to the sofa and sat beside her. Deb patted her lap, and she laid her head in Deb's lap. Deb gently rubbed her fingers through Miranda's hair. "It's okay, Sweetheart. We'll do whatever you say. If you trust her word, we'll trust her word. If you don't, we won't. Right?" Miranda could feel the daggers Deb must have shot at the two men, who just bowed their heads, stopping their argument. She was grateful that Deb was there.

"I trust her," Miranda said, wiping her tears with her hand.

Gavin opened his mouth but shut it again without speaking. He lowered his eyes and nodded. "Okay," he said after several seconds. "I'll trust you and Dan."

Deb's voice softened when she spoke again, "Thank you."

CHAPTER 21

Deb stood and took Gavin by the hand, grabbing her purse and an Escalade key fob. She whispered, "Let's give them some privacy for a little while, Gav."

He nodded in agreement. He waved to Dan, who smiled as he sat on the sofa and hugged Miranda, acknowledging understanding. Then Gavin and Deb walked out the door and down the stairs. Deb had grabbed the key fob to the red Escalade. He helped her into the passenger seat and jogged around to the driver's side, climbing behind the wheel and pushing the start button. He was always such a gentleman, she thought. It was nice, if a little old-fashioned. She smiled at him.

"What?" he said with a laugh.

"You don't want to trust Theo," Deb observed.

"I don't trust Theo. But I trust Dan."

"What happens if he's wrong?"

"Well, we're all only human. Right or wrong, it doesn't matter. Intent is all that really matters, Tish. His intent is to protect his family. It's my duty, as his friend, to respect his choices in how to do that and help him."

Deb smiled again. "You're too good to be true."

He smiled back, "No. I'm really not." He put the SUV in reverse and backed out of the drive.

Deb looked out the passenger side window, seeing the

neighbor staring at them intently, as obvious as she had with Frank and Theo. Deb had no doubt that once they had driven away, the nosy old biddy had tossed down her gardening tools and ran into her own house, calling for her husband, like the next-door neighbor lady on "Bewitched." What was her name? Gladys Kravitz.

Gavin pointed out the car following them as soon as they rounded the first curve. He nodded at the rearview. "Agent Mathews has us under surveillance."

"Are you sure it's the FBI and not somebody...scary?" Deb asked nervously, looking back.

"Yeah, Hon. I saw them last night. They followed our limo from the airport."

"Why didn't you say anything? Does Dan know?"

Gavin smiled. "Dan knows."

The Escalade's navigation system led them to the town of Colonial Beach and through it to the point and the Dockside Restaurant at the yacht club. It was approaching noon, and still a beautiful day, so they decided to get a drink at the tiki bar outside. They parked and found an empty tiki table, a picnic table decorated with palm leaves on the umbrella.

Gavin ordered a Modelo; Deb a glass of merlot. Gavin nodded at the sedan parked in the parking lot. Deb laughed. "You notice everything, huh?"

"Hmmm. Not little boys at the foot of the bed, apparently," he chuckled.

"Can I see your IDs, please?" asked the waitress.

"You're kidding, right?" Deb laughed. "I'm nearly thirty-one."

"Law is to card everyone under thirty-five."

"Hey, no complaints!" Deb laughed, taking her wallet out of her purse and showing her ID. "For the record, though, he's thirty-six."

"Shhhh. Don't take this away from me," Gavin teased, taking out his wallet, his shield showing as he pulled out his driver's license. God, he was handsome. His hair wasn't curly in the way Dan's was, but there was still the hint of curls. He still had a full head of hair, too. It was nearly black and thick. His lashes were long and thick, too, and curtained his golden-brown eyes when he looked down. Even dressed casually, as he was today, he was polished. His clothes were neatly pressed, his boots shined. He wore a tee shirt under a button-down. And he smelled clean, like Irish Spring.

"Thanks. I'll be right back with y'all's drinks," said the waitress with a smile, breaking into Deb's thoughts.

She returned quickly and placed their drinks on the table.

"Can I git y'all anything else?" she asked.

"Not at the moment, thanks," Gavin replied. The girl scurried off to serve another table.

They sat quietly for a few minutes, enjoying the sunshine and watching the boats on the river. Gavin took a swallow of his beer.

Deb looked at Gavin intently. She took a sip of wine, working up courage. "Do you think I'm a slut?" she asked suddenly. She had to know. Was she just another conquest? He could surely have any woman he wanted. That waitress, for example.

"I beg your pardon?" Gavin asked, sounding genuinely surprised.

"It's a simple question. Do you think I'm a slut?" She tried to look casual, but she nervously played with the coaster on the table.

Gavin leaned forward and took her hand. "Deb, I've known you for almost six months. I've spoken to you daily. I've spent entire weekends in your company. In that time, you've only... had relations...with one person. Me. So no, I don't think you're a slut."

"Yeah, but I cheated on my husband with Mark. And Mark just died...six months ago. Plus, we only had relations because I pretty much jumped on top of you. And we did meet once a long time ago when I just walked up and kissed you on a dare." She bit her lip.

Gavin laughed good-naturedly. "Debbie, I was not unwilling. I'd have had relations any time you wanted. As for it only being six months...I don't think there's a clock on grief. You're ready to move on when you're ready. It doesn't mean you didn't love Mark. And as far as the cheating goes, who am I to judge? I didn't know any of you back then. The woman I know today, the woman sitting here, is kind and loyal, not only to me but to the memory of her late boyfriend, her friend Miranda, and HER EX-HUSBAND, who she absolutely adores and wishes nothing but happiness. And as I recall, you gave me a peck on the lips. I kissed you."

"Really?" she asked, her voice cracking, but she smiled sweetly, feeling relieved.

"Yeah, really. I think you're great. I've thought you were great from the moment I met you. Both times."

She looked surprised. "You've liked me...you know, like liked...from the beginning?"

"I've found you attractive from the beginning. I've admired your character from the beginning. I've grown to 'like like' you more every day since. You make me smile, Deb."

She laughed. "I didn't know."

"Well, your boyfriend was shot in the head. And I was investigating his murder. I didn't think it was appropriate to ask you out."

"Did you ask Dan?"

He blushed. "I did."

She widened her mouth into an o. "You didn't?"

He laughed and nodded. "Before Christmas. I didn't want to step on anybody's toes."

"So, why didn't you ask me out?"

"I'm not sure. I kept waiting for the right moment, for a sign you were ready to move on."

"My climbing on your lap wasn't a sign?"

"Hmmm?"

"You still haven't asked me out," she quipped.

"Ms. Bradley, would you like to go to dinner with me when we get home?" he asked.

"Master Sergeant Mahoney, I'd love that." She took a sip of her wine and looked out at the river. "Why didn't you tell me you were Zorro? I know you knew."

"I don't know why I didn't. It just seemed like something I shouldn't bring up until you had a chance to process your grief."

"And it's not slutty that I can't keep my hands off you?"

"You got that same problem with any other guy?" he asked with a wicked gleam in his golden-brown eyes.

"Um, no. I can't say I do," she laughed. She didn't think she'd ever want to kiss anyone else ever again. But she had to fight that urge. Thinking that way got her married to the wrong man and cheating on him with another wrong man. She had to make sure she found the right one before she committed her heart like that.

"Then I don't think you're slutty. I just think you like sex. And I don't have a problem with that."

"Yeah, well. That has a lot to do with you. Cuz. Oh my God!"

He just smiled.

She took another sip of her wine. "I really like you a

lot, Gavin. And I'm totally in for a relationship, not just sex. But I'm not sure I'm ready for forever yet. I kind of rushed into that twice already. The first time, it ended in divorce. The second time ended...well, horribly...but I wasn't completely happy even before."

Gavin smiled. "I'm not ready for forever yet either, Deb. I...I err on the side of caution when it comes to relationships. I'm comfortable with letting you set the pace. We've only known each other for six months. I have no interest in seeing anyone else, but I also have no interest in rushing into a lifetime commitment, either. How about we start at the beginning of the relationship and move forward from here? Really get to know each other?"

"So, you aren't in love with me?" she asked.

"Oh, I am in love with you. I have been since you followed me into that bar. But love doesn't mean we should be married. Marriage takes more than love, Deb." Wasn't that the whole truth? she thought.

She smiled and leaned across the table, kissing him. "I'm in love with you, too. You're the only man who has ever really seen me. All of me. And you never make me feel judged. You let me be myself, have my own interests, show enough interest in them that I can talk about them with you, but not so much that you take them over as your own. And you share in other interests. You're fun to be around. You comfort me when I'm down. You laugh with me when I laugh. And Lord knows you're easy to look at. And like I just said...Oh my God! But you're right. Marriage takes more than love. Thanks for understanding that. At least I know you can wait. You've already waited six months."

"You're worth the wait, Baby," he winked. "Hello, Deputy Juarez." Gavin's attention had not seemed divided, but his powers of observation, a professional attribute, were never "off." He noticed the Deputy, now dressed in jeans and a Kenny Chesney tee shirt, pull in and park his blue F150 pickup and catch sight of them. He was standing at the bar, just ten feet from them.

He smiled and waved, approaching.

"Uh, hello again. How are y'all enjoyin' this weather?"

"It's a beautiful day," Deb agreed.

"Would you care to join us, Deputy?" Gavin asked, motioning for him to have a seat.

"Oh, no. I wouldn't wish to impose," Manny stammered.

"No imposition at all," Gavin replied.

Manny stammered his thanks and sat with them rather nervously, ordering a Miller Lite.

"I just wanted to apologize again for last night's misunderstanding, Sergeant Mahoney," he said as the waitress set his beer on the table.

"Please call me Gavin, and this is Deb. No need to apologize. I've had to do the same. It's not always a comfortable task, especially when the call is motivated by racial...misperceptions."

The Deputy smiled, relieved. "I appreciate your understandin'. And I'm just Manny."

Manny took a large swallow of his beer.

Gavin laughed. "It's okay, Manny. What is it you want to know?"

Manny blushed. "Yeah, I'm a little embarrassed, especially after last night, but my boss wants me to find out what y'all are up to. Apparently, an Agent Thomas Mathews of the FBI paid him a visit this mornin', warning him that y'all are conductin' an unsanctioned manhunt."

"Don't worry, Manny. We aren't going to go outside the law. We're just giving those guys a little unrequested assistance. We'll find him. They'll catch him." Gavin motioned to the sedan in the parking lot.

Manny nodded. "One more thing. My boss wonders where you got all the money you're spending?"

Gavin burst out laughing. "Dan's loaded. He got it the old-fashioned way. He inherited it. His great-grandfather was the founder of Roma Napoli Chicago Pizza."

"Really? I've been to one of those. Good Pizza."

"Yeah, they haven't owned it since the 60s, but he owns a boatload of real estate in Chicago," Deb added.

"How about you?" Manny asked.

Gavin smiled wryly. "What makes you think I have money?"

Manny blushed. "Um…Well, you're wearing an Omega Speedmaster Moon watch. It retails for more than my annual salary."

"It was a gift from my grandfather," Gavin said without even skipping a beat. Deb could swear he was…impressed.

"The last gift my grandfather gave me was a Fuentes International wrench set. Nice, but it didn't cost over $40,000," Manny pushed.

Gavin laughed. He actually laughed. Deb and the deputy were both taken aback by his reaction. He reached into his wallet, pulled out a newspaper clipping, and set it on the table. It was an old clipping with a picture of a man and 4 boys in a parade. Deb and Deputy Juarez leaned in to see. The caption read, "Fuentes International Founder and CEO Enrique Fuentes with grandsons Horatio Fuentes, Frederico Stoke, Gavin Mahoney, and Brandon Kaminski pass out candy at the Fiesta parade."

Deb felt like her head was about to explode. "Holy! Words I'd rather not use. Brandon's my brother. I'm sleeping with you. Neither of you thought to tell me you're rich?"

Gavin laughed harder. "You never asked." When he regained his composure, he asked, "Would you mind keeping that quiet, though. It's not something I exactly advertise."

CHAPTER 22

Pete Camacho stretched and looked out his office window. His first day had started with a terrorist act, with him as the victim. He was an equal measure hero and pariah in the office. It didn't help that his accent was so similar to that of the man who had threatened the safety of them all. The thing was, he was actually good at his job, even in his short tenure. That was obvious to his co-workers. The only way he could make it through was by keeping his head.

He had left his door open every day since Kris Bowen had knocked on it. The sight of it closed, with the possibility of anyone tapping on it, filled him with anxiety. He tried closing it each morning when he arrived in the office, but he found himself unable to let go of the handle and hyperventilating each time. So, instead, he reopened it and shoved the plastic wedge up under the base of the door. Even so, his interactions in the office had been all business. No one reached out to him, and he felt immensely isolated in his office. He was beginning to wonder if that view was worth it.

He glanced at his watch. Ten to twelve. Soon, he'd contemplate whether to eat his lunch alone in his office or alone at a table in the breakroom. Either way, dozens of eyes watched him eat without any of them showing any cordiality. He turned and looked out the glass wall that separated his office from the cubicles beyond and immediately felt the mass return to work. He could close the blinds, but that made him anxious, too. Besides, he didn't want to separate himself from his team further.

Camille suggested he appear more relatable. He had no idea what that even meant. These people had seen him crying, pleading, and afraid. How could they possibly relate to him?

Just as he turned to go back to his seat and refocus his attention on the project he'd been hired to develop, the elevator binged at the far end of the room from his office entrance, and the doors slid open, revealing his gorgeous wife, her creamy light brown skin tone deep and even against the white of the simple cotton dress she was wearing, her hair natural, curly, free brushing her shoulders. Her belly had quickly expanded this time. At six weeks, she was already starting to show, as this was her second pregnancy and third child. Her black patent leather tote was slung over one shoulder, and each arm gracefully hung to her sides and ended in a chubby child clingy sweetly to each hand. Annalise's hair was braided sweetly, and she, too, was dressed in a white dress. She had on little ankle socks with lace trim and little shiny black patent leather Mary Janes. Liam wore a little checked short-sleeve shirt with a little white bow tie, a pair of gray dress slacks, and little black and white wing tips. They could have stepped out of a picture book from the 1960s. He grinned and shook his head. Camille was a trip.

He couldn't help but think of the first time he'd ever laid eyes on her. Spring Break, 2012. Fort Lauderdale. She had walked past him in the hallway of the Holiday Inn, Miranda on one side of her, Mike and Vanessa on the other. She smiled, and they looked back at each other as they passed one another. "Hi there," she had said.

"Hey," he had replied.

He was done for at that moment, in the best possible way.

She threw her shoulders back and prompted her children off the elevator. She smiled and walked confidently across the floor, meandering through the maze of cubicles, making her way to her husband's office. He rose from his chair, walked around his desk, and stood leaning against the doorframe.

"Hey, Baby! Whatchu doin' here?" he asked, kissing her as she sauntered up to him, grinning like a fool. Then he stooped down, grabbing a child in each arm, and lifted them. "Hey, Munchkins. You wanna see where Daddy works?"

They both beamed and squealed in delight.

Margaret Kelso grinned from her desk. She stood up and made her way to her boss's office. "Mr. Camacho, can I get you or your wife some coffee? Or something for those little angels?" she asked. She was his assistant, but it was the first friendly overture she'd made. Pete looked at his wife in shock and surprise. Camille winked at him.

"Oh, no thank you, Margaret. It is Margaret, right?" Camille smiled. "We just came to take our man out to lunch. But thank you."

Margaret smiled back. "Oh, sure! If you need anything, let me know." She waved to the twins. "The kids might enjoy Ed Debevic's. I can reserve a table for you if you like."

"That would be great, Margaret, thank you," Pete replied. "I'm going to give my family the tour. We'll be back in about half an hour, so maybe for 1 pm."

"Yessir," Margaret replied and returned to her desk.

"Baby, you're amazing," Pete grinned, kissing Camille again.

"Ah. I just figured: who could resist those faces?"

CHAPTER 23

Gavin and Deb did some shopping and returned to the beach house with take-out Chinese food for lunch. Despite their earlier conversation, she was cold toward him. As he drove back to the house, Deb sat quietly, staring out the window. "Are you mad at me?" he asked. Damnit, he thought. He should have just told her ages ago, but it never seemed to work out well once he told people. "I'm sorry. If it helps, I'm not rich...exactly. My grandfather is. There's a family trust, but I live on my salary."

"And own $40,000 watches."

"Watch. One watch. And my grandfather did give it to me. I didn't buy it," he argued. It sounded ridiculous. He knew that.

"Why wouldn't you just tell me? It's not like I'm broke. I'm not after your money."

He sighed. "Yeah. I know. I should have. But I just...I don't know how to...I am not that great at talking to people. And I have been burned. All I can say is I'm sorry."

He made the turn onto the lane leading to the house. There was a late model Toyota Camry parked in the driveway.

"Hello," Deb called, walking through the door with her packages. Gavin came in behind her, carrying the Chinese food. Dan and Miranda waved from the balcony. A woman in her mid-fifties was with them. She was plump but not fat, wearing a red sundress with large white polka dots. She wore her brown hair in a short wedge cut. She was smiling and very cute. She waved wildly.

"Ava!" Deb crooned, dropping her bags and rushing to hug the woman.

Gavin followed and placed the food on the table in the sunroom before walking outside to shake Dan's stepmother's hand.

Miranda looked remarkably better than when they had left. Dan still looked worried, but with the arrival of his stepmother, he was starting to relax again. That was good anyway.

Gavin, with Deb ignoring him and not knowing Ava, felt a little as if he were imposing. He decided that he needed some exercise more than lunch and changed into running shorts and shoes. He grabbed a bottle of water and ran down to the beach while the others helped themselves to lunch. He ran as far as he could on the small private beach before turning and running back. He reached the bulkhead on the beach below the balcony and was turning to run the beach again when the neighbor accosted him. She brandished her pruning shears, waving them wildly. She was an older woman, probably in her late sixties. "You! Keep off my beach!" she screamed.

"Oh, I'm sorry. I was just going for a run. I saw other people running this morning," he replied.

"I don't want you people on my beach!" the woman screamed.

"What people?" asked Gavin. "It's just me." He looked around.

Dan came to the side of the balcony and called down, "Everything okay?"

"Yeah. The lady doesn't want me running on her beach. And since I have to cross her section to get to the rest,

I guess I'm done." He turned and climbed the steps, and entered the house. He paced the entry a few times. Finally, he reached down, pulling off his shoes and throwing them into the corner by the door, sand going everywhere. He stared at the mess for a second before getting the broom and dustpan from the closet and sweeping it up.

Deb, who was sitting at the table in the sunroom, rose and walked into the house and up to Gavin. Wordlessly, she took the broom from him. She stood on her tiptoes and wrapped her arms around his neck, hugging him tightly. His arms hung at his sides for a moment before he wrapped them around her waist, hugging her back.

"What a bitch!" she whispered.

He laughed. "Yeah. Unfortunately, she's not alone. There's lots of people like her, Deb. And they live everywhere."

She sighed. "I just wish you hadn't felt the need to hide it from me."

"I didn't. I wear it on my wrist every single day. I just didn't talk about it. If you asked, I'd have told you."

"Told her what?" Miranda asked. He was convinced Miranda had reservations about him. Great, he thought.

Deb held up his wrist. "Do you know what this is?" she asked.

"Sure. It's an Omega Speedmaster. It's a good watch." Miranda answered.

"Any idea how much it costs?" Deb asked, sounding a little surprised.

"About $40,000," Miranda replied.

Gavin snorted.

Ava gasped, "$40,000! For a watch!"

"Well, sure. It's a good watch," she said. She looked like she had no clue that the watch separated him from other people in any way. A watch was just a watch to her.

Dan looked bewildered. "How do you think he could afford a $40,000 watch?" he asked.

"I assume from his trust fund, or it was a gift from his grandfather," she answered. "Why does that matter?"

"Trust fund?" Dan asked.

"It's the latter," Gavin chuckled. "Thanks, Red. Glad at least someone understands it's normal."

"Wait. You knew he was walking around with $40,000 in jewelry on him?" Deb demanded.

"Well, it's not like he's hiding it. It's on his wrist, for Pete's sake."

"How'd you know it was a gift from his grandfather?" Dan asked, starting to laugh.

"Because his grandfather is Enrique Fuentes...Isn't he?" She was starting to sound a little confused herself.

"He is." Gavin laughed. Thank God. Now, they would see. Money was just money. It wasn't something you needed to talk about. It didn't make the person any better or worse. And oddly, the one person here who liked him the least was the one to see it.

"Why wouldn't you say you had money?" Dan laughed.

"I told you I don't tell people how much I have..." Gavin said.

"I thought you were joking."

"Oh. I wasn't."

Deb's phone rang. She released Gavin and pulled her phone from her pocket. "Ha. Speaking of money. It's my bank," she said, answering the call. "Hello. – This is she. – What? – I am in Virginia, but I haven't used my card at all. – Are you kidding me? – No. None of that was me. – Yeah. Thank you. – Yes, give me a second. I'll look."

Gavin asked. "What's up?"

"Fraud protection. There's been a bunch of charges on my Visa card in Virginia," she answered, grabbing her purse and taking out her wallet. "Damnit. The card's missing. I must have lost it at the tiki bar. It's the only place I had my wallet out. You paid for everything with the cash *Dan* gave you."

"He told me to!"

"He thought you were poor."

"Again! No one asked."

"I'm sorry. I just don't understand why you're upset," Miranda said to Deb.

"He's rich. He didn't trust me to tell me."

"What? I...I'm going to disagree. I just don't think the fact that he has money matters to him. I don't see that telling somebody something they can clearly see is trust. He's more than showed you trust in other ways."

"Says the girl who buys a house with cash. They live in a different world than us, Deb," Dan said.

"Lived. You're in it now, too. Remember who threw a stack of cash at whom."

CHAPTER 24

Returning from lunch, Camille, despite being tired, insisted on walking Pete back to his office, convincing him that the visual of him with his family one more time would soften more of his co-workers' blockade against him. She promised him she'd rest when she got home when she got the twins down for a nap. She'd left her tote in his office just so she'd have an excuse to walk the children through one more time.

She had forgotten to account for her feet swelling and the children being cranky. It was a far less successful parade than the original. After getting her bag and kissing her husband goodbye, she turned to leave, losing hold of Liam's hand as they nearly reached the elevator. Pete watched his son jut off down the hallway to the left of the elevators.

Camille gave chase, but the boy made it into a records room. While most work was performed digitally, even robotics designs were printed on blueprints. Liam laughed as he burst into the room, surprising a clerk who was hard at work. Camille snatched him up, apologizing profusely. "I'm so sorry," she exclaimed.

The clerk, Ivan Polaski, a chubby man in his mid-sixties, laughed jovially. "Oh, he can't hurt anything. I'm just pulling obsolete designs to be sent to storage."

She wrangled the squirming boy onto her hip, letting go of Annalise momentarily. The girl chose that moment to knock several tubes off the counter. "Annalise!"

Pete ran in behind Camille and grabbed Annalise. "Sorry, Ivan!" Thank God for that man. What would she do without his steady, loving influence?

"Bowen Tobacco?" Camille asked, picking up one of the tubes, noting the label.

"Um, yes. I believe it's old plans for automation at an e-cig manufacturing plant. Obsolete now. This is a good twenty years old," Ivan answered conversationally.

Camille grabbed Pete's arm, trying to beam her thoughts to him telepathically. Bowen Tobacco...Bowen Tobacco,..Bowen Tobacco.

"Bowen Tobacco is a client?" Pete asked. "I haven't seen a file for them." Good. He got the message.

"Oh, no. Not currently. Like I said, this is probably twenty years old. But Mr. Moore was good friends with the Bowens, once upon a time."

"The other day. The bomb. That was Kris Bowen," Pete said.

"Was it really? I had the day off. Thank God! I wasn't even here. It must have been awful."

CHAPTER 25

Dan stood on the balcony looking out over the river. Poor Danny. He was so confused. Personally, she couldn't understand what either he or Deb was so upset about. Had they seriously not noticed his clothes, the watch, or the words he used? Like whom. Who says whom? Miranda thought. Besides Mike, that is.

Miranda walked up behind Dan and kissed his shoulder, wrapping her arms around his waist. He rubbed her arm. "What are you thinking?" she asked.

"That I don't understand your world of privilege. But he's right. I tossed a stack of cash at him…like it was nothing… because it was nothing. In five months, a stack of cash went from life-altering to nothing. He spent my stack because it didn't matter. If he'd spent his, it wouldn't have mattered. Who the hell are we?"

She nodded and laid her head against his back. "You're still you, Danny. You're just you, wealthy. He never said he was rich. But he never said he was poor, either. And he doesn't exactly walk, talk, or dress like a poor man. Ever been to his house?"

Dan nodded. "Top of the line. Everything. Not necessarily the most fashionable, but everything from his pots and pans to his electronics are the best you can get. And it's all expensive. Some investigator I am," he laughed.

"Don't be stupid. You just saw your friend. You didn't question it. You just accepted it for what it was. That's who you are."

That's when her phone rang. She pulled it out of her back pocket and looked at it. The caller ID read, "Unidentified Number."

"Dan!" she gasped, fear filling her again as she showed him the phone.

"Answer it. On speaker," he commanded, motioning for Deb to stay quiet, who walked out onto the balcony as Miranda was answering her phone.

"Hello?" Miranda said, holding the phone out so Dan could hear.

"Hello, Miranda. It's good to see you. You look well," Kris's voice said.

"What do you want, Kris?"

"I want you to pay for what you did."

"What I did?"

"You killed my baby, Miranda."

"I miscarried, not that it's any of your business. You have no claim to any part of my life. Not then. Not now. I planned to give it up for adoption. I want no part of you." she said, fear replaced by anger.

"I saw you go into that clinic."

"Yeah, I went. And I left. Besides, didn't your daddy tell you to stay away from me?"

"My daddy is no longer able to tell me what to do."

"Your daddy was so disappointed in you, Kris."

"Don't you talk about my daddy, you whore."

"I don't take orders from you, Kris. I'm not drugged," she spat.

Gavin emerged from the shower and walked onto the balcony, drying his hair with a white towel.

"Your Mexican friend should hang that towel up so it doesn't mildew. Of course, you should wash it first. In case the white is stained from that brown skin."

Then he hung up.

"He can see us," Dan said, looking around. There were a few boats on the river, but they were in motion. The beach itself was unoccupied, being too early for swimmers. A neighbor down the beach was fishing off his pier, but he was clearly an older, overweight man. Gavin and Dan both turned to look at the yacht club.

"He's not at that cabin," Gavin said. She noticed he didn't say that he told them so. But he'd told them so.

"Nope," Dan replied.

"Not much use in going there." Gavin acknowledged.

"Next to none."

"So, you don't."

"We don't."

Gavin looked down. "I'll go home if you want me to."

Dan cocked his head to the side. "Why would I want you to go home? Seems to me I got no right to be pissed at you for not telling me something that should have been obvious."

CHAPTER 26

Deb looked across at the yacht club as well. "I don't know if this has anything to do with anything, but I didn't lose my card over there."

Everyone turned to look at her. Gavin looked positively pitiful, especially.

"Or at least, the charges started before we left Chicago. Somebody bought an airline ticket on American Airlines in my name from Chicago to Baltimore International yesterday morning. And it wasn't me."

Dan closed his eyes and sighed. "Where's Bob?"

"I thought of that. I called Brandon. Uncle Bob is with them. He was sitting with him at their kitchen table. Melissa didn't want him lurking and just invited him in," Deb replied.

"Here's where I ask if they have garlic," Dan snickered.

Deb rolled her eyes. "Here's the thing. I know I had it yesterday morning. I used it at Target. And when I used it, I just threw it into my purse, since we were getting ready to come here. When I got home, I pulled it out of my purse and put it back into my wallet."

"No. You don't think? They'd have called," Gavin said. He knew exactly what she thought. She was certain. He knew everything she thought. Always.

"They called," she replied. "While we were in the air. I never checked my missed calls or voicemail."

"Damnit!" Dan exclaimed.

"What?" Miranda asked, confused.

"My mom," Deb replied. She called her sister, Katelynn. "Hey, kiddo. – Yeah, I know. - You're there now? – I'm sorry you have to deal with this. – What did they say? – They didn't notice she was gone? – Well, what were they doing for 6 hours? – Yeah, I know. – Therapeutic excursions are part of her program. – Yeah, I think she followed me on my vacation. – She stole my credit card and has been using it near where I'm staying. Well, I assume it's her. It disappeared about the same time she did. – Yeah, I'll call the Center. Thanks, Babe. - Love you, too. Bye." Deb disconnected and called the Warden's office at the psychiatric detention center where her mother was supposed to be serving out her sentence for arson. She gave them all the information she had and advised them that she had not seen her mother but suspected she had stolen her card and followed her to Virginia. She sighed, advising them she understood that a BOLO would be issued.

"We can probably expect another visit from the sheriff's department," she huffed after she hung up.

"Come on, Deb. Let's take a walk. Please," Gavin suggested, giving Deb a look. It melted her resolve.

Dan nodded. "Miranda, honey, let's get out of Kris's line of vision, okay?"

"He will not force me to hide, Dan."

Dan pulled her into his arms. "I'm not asking you to hide because you should be afraid of him. I'm asking so we can have time to formulate a plan to locate him. He doesn't need to see our every move. That's all," he said. Damn men. She watched as Miranda's resolve melted, too.

Miranda sighed and kissed him deeply, melting into his embrace. "Okay, for you, because you asked so nicely."

They all headed into the house. Dan lowered the blinds

in the sunroom and throughout.

Gavin took Deb's hand, and they headed out the door. Her heart skipped a beat.

Dan looked at Miranda. He smiled at her, took her hand, and led her toward the stairs.

"I thought you wanted to think," she said, laughing.

"I can't think right now," he replied with a silly grin.

She laughed. "Is there anything I can do to help?"

"Oh, yes. As a matter of fact," he said, pulling her close again.

Deb turned stopped, and when Gavin turned to look at her, she asked, "Do you trust me?"

"Yes," he said. There was honesty in his face. He looked her directly in the eyes. I don't tell people...anything really. Because when I do, I...lose them. I...I'm a harbinger."

Holy crap! He's serious, she thought.

"Who broke you?" she whispered.

He closed his eyes. "Life broke me, DeBella. I'm 36 years old, and anytime I feel a little happy, I just know the bottom is going to drop out from under me. Because it always does."

"We're at the beginning of this relationship, right? Tell me as little as you want. Just tell eventually."

"Deal," he agreed, smiling finally.

CHAPTER 27

Gavin and Deb walked out onto the main street away from the river. The neighbor had followed at what she thought was a discreet distance. Gavin and Deb ignored her.

There was on one side a bit of marshy land and woods on the other side. They walked up around a blind curve. The sedan was parked in a small dirt turnaround bordering the marshy patch.

Holding Deb's hand, Gavin walked up to the sedan and knocked on the window. Special Agent Mathews lowered the window and peered at Gavin over his Ray Bans.

"I really think you'd be more comfortable in the house, Agent Mathews," Gavin said.

"How long have you known I was here?"

"We saw you following us last night. And again this morning. And on the way back," Gavin smiled.

"You're a good cop, Sergeant Mahoney. Don't go messing up your life."

"I don't plan to. Neither does Dan. We didn't have anything you didn't until a minute ago."

"What do you have?"

"Kris Bowen just called Miranda. He could see us. Made a xenophobic comment about the towel I was using. We think he's at the yacht club."

Agent Mathews nodded. "What about the young

trophy wife?"

"Dan thinks he's more preoccupied with Miranda than worried about Theo. Personally, I think she's dangerous, too. She's not smart, exactly. But she didn't marry the old man just to be cut out so easily. She'll get what she wants. I'm just not sure what that is. I haven't looked at the 'proof' that he paid someone to tamper with his brother's car, but I'm sure it's inconclusive, or she wouldn't have been at our door."

"Yeah. It's damning enough to get the old man to disinherit him but nothing to convict him of any crime. The vehicle was in working order. Nothing wrong with the brakes or any other part of the vehicle. His blood alcohol was twice the legal limit. He got drunk. He got lucky and only killed himself," Agent Mathews confirmed. "We have Kris on the explosives and kidnapping, though."

"Heads up, Deb's mom escaped, and we think she's looking for him. He threatened her grandson. Then he kidnapped him. After what she's been through, she's a bit of a wild card."

"Yeah, I read the file. What about the brothers?"

"Well, the brother slash cousin slash, I don't even want to think about it, is in prison. Frank is with Theo, and Bob is with Jason in Sterling, Illinois. Hey, what's with telling the Sheriff we're conducting an unsanctioned manhunt?" Gavin laughed.

"Had to tell him something," the older man snorted, "after the bigoted neighbor called the police on you."

"Yeah, she's a peach. She's right over there behind that tree, by the way."

Deb stood looking at Gavin with her mouth hanging open. She had just told him he could tell her things in his own time. Why was she glaring at him like that? She turned quickly to see the neighbor hiding behind the tree, taking video with her phone. "Hey!" she called out.

The woman turned to run when another agent came up behind her, identified himself, and took her phone, deleting the video.

"I'm not a drug dealer, Mrs. Hogue. I'm a police officer," Gavin said without looking at her.

"Oh. Um. I...Well, what am I supposed to think?" she huffed. "How do you know my name?"

"It's on your mailbox, and I can read," he replied, snidely.

Deb burst out laughing. Okay. She was okay. She wasn't leaving. The bottom hadn't dropped out.

CHAPTER 28

Miranda lay beside Dan. "I'm sorry," she whispered. She was mortified.

"What for?" he asked, rubbing her arm.

"For…not…"

"Don't be silly," Dan smiled.

She sniffed and turned away from him.

"Hey. Miranda. We never have to do anything you don't want to do. Never. I hope you know that," he said, laying his hand on her shoulder.

"I do. But still. I…hate to disappoint you."

He laughed. "You could never disappoint me."

"Why do you love me?" she asked with a giggle.

"I don't know. Because I can't see a future without you, I guess," he said, kissing her shoulder.

She rolled back to face him, widening her eyes. "That's a really great answer!"

He smiled back at her. "It's the truth."

"Okay. So, when did you first start loving me?"

"When you explained to Mike why your mom was so upset when she couldn't find him that very first day."

"No. I'm serious."

"So am I. I told my dad that night I was going to marry you. He said he approved, but I should wait until we were at least six."

"I thought you saw me as Mike's annoying sister," she said.

"I did. It was a love/hate relationship," he guffawed. "Now, as for when I started to understand that I loved you more than hated you, that is, maybe it was when you kicked Wendy Welker in the shins."

"Hah! Which time?"

"Good point. No. No. I know when it was. Freshman year in high school. Mike, you, and I all had freshman English together, first period. Remember?"

"Ah. Yes. Wayne Carver. Poor kid."

"Yeah. One of the few times I'd ever seen Mike show emotion. I mean outside a panic attack."

"I know what you mean. His panic attacks were… sort of anti-emotion. They were what happened when he was afraid he wouldn't be able to control his emotions or didn't understand his emotions. They weren't the actual emotion itself. You're right. Mike's reaction to Wayne Carver's suicide was actual emotion. I think he saw himself in Wayne a little."

"Ms. Jacobson told the class Wayne had taken his own life the night before. Naturally, everyone was quiet. Even Wendy Welker and Caroline Fuller, for a change. But Mike started crying. I'd never seen him cry before," Dan said. "But what I remember most was you. You stood up, walked over to Mike, wiped his tears, and told him it was okay to cry. Crying was part of being human, and Wayne deserved someone crying for him. Mike said he wished he'd known Wayne was so sad that he would have done something to help him. You wiped the hair out of his face and said you know he would have tried because he had such a big heart, but there is no 'what if,' only 'what is.' He couldn't change what had happened, but he could help keep Wayne's memory alive and help make sure no other kid like him felt that way again."

"You knew you loved me more than hated me because I comforted my brother in class?"

"No," he laughed heartily. "I knew I loved you more than hated you because you helped your brother found the 'You're Never Alone' teen suicide prevention initiative at the high school, an initiative you still fund. You both followed through. You weren't just saying words. You were making commitments."

She smiled. "How do you know I still fund it?"

He winked. "I'll never tell."

"You saw the letter from the new principal last month, didn't you?"

"You left it out on the desk."

"So, what did you do about it?" she asked suspiciously.

"Absolutely nothing. That's between you and your brother. I wouldn't take it or the pleasure of providing it from you for the world. If you wanted my money or my help, you'd ask for it. Other than my normal annual contribution and sharing the email that was sent to me from the student chairman to literally everybody, including my new contacts, I did nothing."

"That's how I met Sally Blevins, you know."

"No. How so?"

"I was looking for someone to help us, and Mike suggested Sally. She was in one of his AP classes. I grabbed her walking out of class one day, and told her I was taking her to lunch off campus. I shocked her into agreeing. Mike and I took her to White Castle, explained the idea to her, and asked her to act as Publicity Coordinator," she sighed. "She's been a good friend."

"Okay, my love, your turn. When did you know you loved me?"

"Well, it wasn't that first day. I actually waited until

we were six. And it wasn't any one particular moment. It was how sad you were and how you just accepted everyone, especially Mike, just as they were. How you never saw him or me as less than?"

"Why would I see either of you as less than? You were both more than," he asked, perplexed.

She kissed him. "There. That. Right there. I wish I was half as good as you see me as."

"Back at ya. But you know what? Together, we're almost there."

She sighed and laid her head on his chest. He wrapped his arms around her and kissed the top of her head.

Deb's voice called out from downstairs, "Miranda! Where are you?"

"Up here!" Miranda called back.

"Everybody decent?" Deb asked.

"Yes, come on up," Miranda said, sitting up.

Deb came upstairs. "Did you know these two are working with Agent Mathews?" she asked with her hand on her hip.

"No! That jackass?"

Dan laughed. "He's a good agent. He and your dad asked us to help."

"My dad?" Miranda exclaimed. "That's why he didn't object. I knew he was too much of a control freak to just let me come here without a fight." She picked up a pillow and smacked Dan with it. "What am I? Bait?"

"Well, yeah. But that was the case whether or not Agent Mathews was involved."

"Ugggg!" she groaned, trying to get up.

But he grabbed her hand and pulled her back. "Hey, I love you. Now and forever. And I won't put you in danger. Ever. The best way to protect you is to catch this guy. I can't live without you. I was dead serious when I said I can't see a future without you. Please, trust me."

"I do trust you," she whispered. He kissed her. She let him, despite being miffed at being used as bait.

CHAPTER 29

Deb headed back downstairs to find Gavin had gone out onto the balcony and was staring out at the river. She felt she needed a minute and went instead into the bedroom they were sharing. He was infuriating. He was fragile in some ways. She'd listened to Miranda talking to Dan, and she had to admit what she'd said had made sense. But his communication skills really sucked. She sat down on the bed and looked around the room. He was impossibly neat. She felt like going into his drawer and unfolding everything. She stood up again, walked over to the dresser, and pulled open the drawer. As she expected, everything was neatly folded and arranged by color. So much so that she actually laughed. He was too cute to stay mad at.

"You really like him, don't you?" came her mother's voice from behind her.

She looked up in the mirror. Her mother stood in the now-open Jack and Jill bathroom's sliding door into the bedroom.

"Mom! What are you doing?" she exclaimed. "You can't just walk out of the mental institution."

Kathy laughed. "I think I proved that I can."

"And you can't just break into houses. Mine included."

Kathy shrugged and motioned to the room. "Again, I think I can. My dad taught me."

She walked into the room and sat down on the bed, patting it. "Come. Sit with me for a minute before your police officer misses you."

Deb sighed and sat beside her mother, giving her a hug.

Kathy smiled and brushed Deb's hair out of her eyes. "You look at this one the right way."

"What does that mean?" Deb laughed.

"Oh, I don't know. Like you mean it. Like the redhead looks at him," she answered, nodding at the ceiling.

Deb blushed. "Do you think so? Really?"

Kathy nodded. "And he looks at you the same way. He isn't who I would have chosen, but if history has proven anything, it's my choices in that arena are really bad. I'm sorry I was so hard on the redhead. She's been to see me several times, you know?"

"No. I didn't."

"She's actually quite nice. She treated me like a person, not the crazy bitch who tried to scare her."

"Yeah, I like her. She's really great with Jason, too. She doesn't try to override me or replace me. And she loves him."

"Which him?" her mother quipped.

"Both of them," she smiled.

"And you don't want him anymore?"

"I don't want to be with him anymore. I'll always love him, though. He gave me Jason."

"How did you grow up so well? I never did," Kathy observed sadly.

"You kept the bad stuff well hidden, Mom. So did I. But I never doubted your love. I never will."

"That evil man said he'd hurt Jason," Kathy said, changing the subject. "I won't allow that."

"Jason's okay, Mom. He's with Brandon. Dad's son."

"I know who Brandon is, dear. And I know he's a good man. Better than his father. Better for not having known him. But I'm glad Boban is there. I don't trust the evil man. The redhead should be careful."

"She has a name."

Kathy smiled. "Miranda should be careful. He's really evil. Dark evil. Like my baba. I'll take care of it."

"Mom, leave it to the FBI. You need to go back. Please."

"I'm not going back, dear. I'm never getting better." She kissed Deb on the forehead and stood.

Deb reached out to grab her, trying to keep her there, wanting her mother to return to the mental health facility, but she slipped free and disappeared into the Jack and Jill bath.

"Mom!" she yelled, racing after her. The door was locked. She banged on it. "Mom!"

Gavin came running inside. Dan and Miranda bounded down the stairs.

Deb banged and kicked the door. "Mom! Please! Mom!"

Dan ran out the door and down the steps, looking frantically around the house and in the garage. Gavin ran into the other bedroom. He opened the sliding door on that side and unlocked the bath door into his and Deb's room. Kathy was gone.

CHAPTER 30

Pete was late getting home. It was already dark outside when he walked into his front door, a townhouse two doors down from Miranda and Dan's. Camille was lying on the sofa. He sat down, and she propped her swollen feet into his lap. He gently rubbed them.

"Ahhhhh!" she sighed. "You're a good man, Pete Camacho."

He grunted in response.

"What is it, Baby?" she asked, closing her eyes, thankful that he was home. The twins had been down for about half an hour, but they had refused to nap, and she had never recovered from the trip to Chicago. Her knees ached, and her feet were killing her.

"I'm not really sure," he answered. "I had coffee with Ivan and Margaret this evening before I came home."

"That's great. More and more people will start coming around. You'll see."

"Oh, yeah. The afternoon was much better. But that's not what I'm talking about."

"Then what?" she asked. "Don't forget the ankles."

He rubbed her ankles. "I got the story from Margaret and Ivan. They've both been with the company for forever. Well, my boss, Benjamin Moore, III is CEO, but he doesn't own the company. He's old Chicago money. His father, who's in his 90s, still owns everything. And he inherited it from his father. They're on par with the Genelis, or more accurately, with Dominic Ricardi."

"So, they knew Dan's biological grandmother? Ahhhhh. That's soooo good."

"Yeah. They knew her. Here's the thing. Benjamin Moore, II, my boss's father, left academia to take over his father's businesses when his father, the first Benjamen Moore, died in 1966. My boss was ten at the time," he continued.

"Okay? What's bothering you about that?"

"Well, Benjamin Moore, II taught American Literature...at the University of Illinois, Champaign from 1962 through 1966."

He stopped rubbing. Camille sat up, putting her feet on the floor.

"You're fucking kidding!"

"Nope. I think I found out who Dan's maternal grandfather is. And maybe that's why I was hired when his name came up. And with the connection my boss has to the Bowens...maybe this isn't about Miranda, or not at least all about Miranda," he said, looking intently at his wife. "And here's what's weird. I did some digging in the records myself. Those plans. They weren't twenty years old. They were almost twenty-six years old. Geneli Architecture had the contract to design the plant for Bowen Tobacco, where those robotics from Moore were to be installed. Everything fell apart in September, 1998. Benjamin Moore, II demanded Moore Robotics drop the project the day after Ellen and Carrie Bradley were murdered. And he issued a ban on working with either Geneli Architecture or Bowen Tobacco from that point onward. That's a weird coincidence, right?"

"I'd say!" Camille responded. "You have to call Dan."

CHAPTER 31

Miranda pushed her plate away. "Ug. I don't think I can eat another bite. The crabcakes are amazing, though," she sighed.

Deb smiled weakly, pushing the crabcake around on her plate. She'd barely taken two bites. "It's good. I'm just worried about my mother."

Miranda reached across the table and took her hand. "I know. I'm worried about her, too. But Agent Mathews will make sure they are gentle with her."

Gavin waved down the waitress. "Check, please, and can we have something to take this home?" The four of them had driven around to Dockside Restaurant from their VRBO house for dinner.

Dan's phone rang. His brows knit together. "Pete," he said, pushing back his chair and walking out to the deck to take the call.

Miranda smiled. "I'm going to run to the restroom while he's gone."

"I don't know if that's a good idea! Kris Bowen has a boat docked here!" Gavin interrupted.

Miranda rolled her eyes. "Look. There's the bathroom door. Right there. You can watch me go in. I'll check if anybody's in there before I close the door."

She threw her napkin on her plate and made a show of verifying the bathroom was empty before walking inside and allowing the door to close behind her. She took care of her business. When she came out of the stall, Kathy Kaminski was standing there, waiting for her.

"Ahhhhh! Geez. Mrs. Kaminski! You startled me. I didn't hear you come in. Deb's worried about you!" Miranda exclaimed.

"She can stop worrying now," she said cryptically. "Tell her I won't be coming into her house anymore. Or yours. I promise. When last we spoke, she told me I couldn't do it anymore."

"Okay. But you should tell her. She's just outside in the dining room."

Kathy shook her head. "You're a nice girl, Miranda Davis. I'm sorry I misjudged you. Just tell my girls I love them."

Miranda turned to quickly wash her hands. She turned on the water and soaped them. "You need to go back, Mrs. Kaminski…Mrs. Kaminski?" As she looked in the mirror, she saw only the door closing. She was alone in the restroom.

She quickly rinsed her hands and flung the water off, not bothering to dry them. She hurried out the door and looked around. No Kathy.

She ran out in a hurry, and Gavin jumped up. She ran back to the table. "Didn't you see her? Kathy was in the restroom. She was talking to me. Then, when I turned around to wash my hands, she left. You had to see her!"

Gavin shook his head. "I didn't see anyone go in or out after you went in."

Deb jumped up. "Maybe she went into a stall!"

She and Miranda ran back to the restroom. They checked all the stalls. It was empty.

"I swear to God, Deb. She was here!"

"She was here," Deb agreed, squatting and picking up

her missing credit card off the floor. "What did she say?"

"It was weird. She said she wouldn't be sneaking into your house again, or mine, that you'd told her she couldn't do it anymore. Then she said she was sorry she'd misjudged me and that I should tell you and Katelynn she loves you."

Deb went pale. "Damnit," she cried, tears filling her eyes. "She never plans on coming home...alive."

Miranda looked at her, puzzled.

"I disinvited her in."

"What? She thinks she's a vampire?"

Deb shook her head. "No, she thinks she'll be a vampire, a mulla, actually. But since we're ethnic Transylvanian Romani, it amounts to the same thing in her mind. It's what her doctor calls a 'persistent delusion.'" Her tears fell down her cheeks. Miranda took her hands, pulled her to stand, and hugged her. Hard.

When they opened the door, Dan and Gavin were waiting just outside the door.

"She's gone. But Miranda was right. She was there," Deb said, holding up the credit card.

"What did Pete want?" Miranda asked, slipping her arm through Dan's.

"To tell me that my mother's father is probably Benjamin Moore, II. Oh, and that the Bowens and Genelis and Moores were all connected in business until the day after Geno killed my mother and sister when Bennie boy suddenly cut all ties with both businesses, costing all three families millions."

"What does that mean?" Miranda asked.

"It means we're going home," he replied.

As they walked out to the silver Escalade, there was a commotion in the yacht club. A boat sped out of the bay and into the river. Deb stopped and grabbed Gavin's hand. "Mom," she whispered.

A woman came running down the dock to the parking lot. "There's a woman in the water! I think she's dead! Somebody call 911!"

Miranda took out her phone and called. Dan and Gavin ran down the dock in the direction the woman had come. They both stopped near a boat named "Dominica's Dream." They knelt down. Dan lay prone on the dock, reaching down into the bay beside the boat, and he and Gavin pulled the woman onto the dock.

Gavin pulled off his jacket, rolling it up, and placed it like a pillow beneath the woman's head. Dan pulled his belt off and tightened it around the woman's leg, obviously as a tourniquet. The woman grasped Dan's arm and shoved something into his hand. A crowd had gathered around them by this point. The woman gasped and shuddered. Gavin suddenly started CPR. Miranda gave the information to the emergency dispatch on the line and held Deb as she cried.

Miranda saw the flash from Dan's camera as he took a picture of whatever the woman had thrust into his hand as the police and ambulance arrived.

The woman who had come running down the dock sat on a curb, rocking back and forth. "Is she dead? Oh my God! Is she dead?"

Deb looked imploringly at Miranda. "Is it my mom, Randi?" she whispered, wringing her hands.

"I…I think so, Honey. It's hard to tell from here." But Miranda knew it was Kathy. What's more, she was sure Deb knew it, too.

Deb buried her face in Miranda's shoulder and sobbed.

CHAPTER 32

Kathy had been stabbed seven times. Additionally, her leg had been slashed from the femoral artery to just above the knee. Dan had pulled the belt as tight as he could, but she'd already lost too much blood by the time they'd pulled her out of the water. She'd thrust the letter into his hands and whispered, "Jason. Not safe. You. Not safe." Then, she lost consciousness just before Gavin started administering CPR. He was unable to resuscitate her.

Dan, seeing the flashing lights, quickly snapped a few pictures of the soggy paper. The ink was running, but it was still legible. Dan gasped at the sight of Mike's neat signature blurred at the bottom of the typewritten page, clearly bearing the watermark of Park, Davis, and Feldman, Attorneys at Law. He knew he'd have to hand the letter over to the police arriving on the scene, but he wasn't going to hand it over without an opportunity to read it more thoroughly. At a glance, it appeared to be the cover letter to a will Mike had drawn up for a client, dated January 31, 2022. Dan shuddered as déjà vu flooded his brain. The letter was addressed to Benjamin Alexander Moore II at his residence in Chicago. *What was Kathy doing with it in Virginia? Did she die getting it? Next to a 1969 Chris Craft cabin cruiser named "Dominica's Dream"?*

The EMTs took over from Gavin but quickly declared

Kathy DOA. Colonial Beach Police took over and took statements from everyone at the scene. Dan told them what she had said to him and handed over the letter. He pointed out the boat and explained the significance of the name Dominica, being his biological maternal grandmother's name. He laid out the whole story, everything they'd been through over the last six months, how Kathy had disappeared, how Mark had been killed, how Kris Bowen had kidnapped Jason and begun stalking Miranda, about Miranda's history with the man.

"Somehow, it's all connected. I don't know how. But it is," he explained.

Once the police had corroborated the story with the Kane County Sheriff, they were all allowed to go back to the beach house.

"You have my mother's blood all over you," Deb said softly, looking at Gavin, who was indeed covered in blood from his attempts to resuscitate Kathy. She plopped down on the sofa, looking away.

"Um. Yeah, I guess I do," he replied, looking at his hands and clothes. "I'll go take a shower," he continued after a long awkward silence.

Dan nodded. "Me too. Miranda, can you sit with Deb for a few minutes?" He was also covered in Kathy's blood, but Deb didn't seem to notice.

Miranda sat down beside Deb and put her arm around Deb's shoulder, giving it a squeeze. "Sure. We'll sit here together. We can talk…or not. Whatever you want, Deb."

"I'm okay, Randi. I am. Can you call Uncle Frank for me? I'll call Katelynn."

She turned away from Gavin. He felt the sting of it. He shifted his weight on his feet and looked at the floor. Dan put his hand on his shoulder.

"Give her a few minutes. You got the worst of it. You're

a bit grisly to look at right now," he whispered to his friend.

******

Gavin nodded and looked down at his clothes and hands. He'd been avoiding looking. He had a flash of desert camos covered in blood. He went to the kitchen, grabbing a trash bag from under the sink for his clothes. He never wanted to see them again. Then he went into the bedroom and into the Jack and Jill bath.

He rinsed his watch in the sink. Then he dropped it in the trash bag. He looked at his reflection in the mirror. His 24-year-old self stared back at him. First Lieutenant Gavin Mahoney, 82nd Airborne.

He started the shower as he peeled his blood-soaked clothing off and threw them into the trash bag. Even his shoes and underwear went in the bag with the watch. He climbed into the shower and scrubbed. He scrubbed and rinsed over and over, but every time he looked down, he saw the desert camos covered in blood.

******

Dan grabbed a trash bag, but he headed upstairs to the master bath.

"I'll call anybody you want me to call, Honey," Miranda said, hugging Deb.

Deb made the call to her sister. The two cried together for the next half an hour.

"Gavin tried for a long time to resuscitate her. They had to pull him away," she told her sister.

Suddenly, Deb sat bolt upright and turned to look at the bedroom door that Gavin had disappeared through. "Katelynn, I love you. But I have to go. I owe somebody an apology. I just treated Gavin like a pariah. – Yes. Oh, that would be nice. Please call them. – I'll call you tomorrow."

She disconnected the call and looked at Miranda, "I

hurt him, didn't I?"

Miranda stammered, "Um, no. I mean, I'm sure he understands."

Deb kissed her cheek. "You're a terrible liar."

She stood up and went into the bedroom. Gavin was still in the shower. She knocked softly on the bathroom door.

"Yeah, I'll be out in a minute!" he called.

She slid the door open a crack. "I'm so sorry, Gavin."

"Oh, it's okay, Honey. I was hard to look at, I'm sure," he answered.

She pushed the door all the way open and entered, leaning against the wall. "No, I was just in shock, I think. You tried to save her. I don't ever want to treat you like that. I don't ever want this kind of distance between us. I love you."

He shut off the water and grabbed a towel, wrapping it around his waist. He stepped out of the shower and smiled. "It's okay. I love you, too, and I understand."

She flung her arms around his neck and hugged him as he grabbed the towel to keep from losing it.

"You got me at a bit of a disadvantage here, Honey," he laughed.

"Jesus, Babe. You aren't supposed to scrub off skin," she said, noting where he'd scrubbed his chest raw.

"Oh. I didn't notice," he said, looking down.

"Put on some pants and come out. I'll put some salve on that," she said, kissing his cheek.

"It's okay. Really."

"Gavin. Come out, and I'll put some salve on that."

"Okay," he agreed begrudgingly.

She left the bathroom and went to the supply closet in the kitchen. "Hey, Miranda, where's that first aid kit? I thought I saw it in here."

"Um, yeah. I think Dan moved it to the top shelf."

Deb looked up. "Yeah, I'll need a ladder."

Miranda snorted. "Dan, come get that first aid kit for Deb!"

He came down the stairs. "What?"

Deb answered and pointed. "First aid kit."

"Oh, sorry. Sure." He walked over and reached over her head, and took it down for her.

She took it back into the bedroom. Behind her, Dan sat down beside Miranda.

Gavin emerged shirtless from the bathroom and sat on the bed as Deb applied the salve. She gently rubbed each scar of the dozen or so small scars peppering his chest and right shoulder. He closed his eyes at her gentle touch. Gavin never spoke. When she was done, he grabbed a shirt and pulled it on. He walked out, still without having spoken. He walked right out past Dan and Miranda without speaking. He went to the balcony and stood watching the river.

Deb followed him out, placing the first aid kit on the kitchen island.

She stood beside him, leaning on the balcony half-wall. After several moments of silence, he said, "It's a Lady Macbeth thing, Deb. Some blood doesn't wash away so easily. Just know it has nothing to do with you."

"Okay," she said. She took his hand and interlocked her fingers with his. They just stood there looking at the river. He pulled her hand to his chest and closed his eyes. "I'm not going anywhere," she whispered. He turned to her and kissed her. She had never felt so needed in her life.

"Tell me about your mom," he said as he pulled away, staring directly into her soul with those eyes.

She looked down, the grief flooding her heart. "She was...hard to ignore." She laughed, remembering her mother. "She used to play dress-up with me. She made all the costumes. She taught me to sew and to crochet. And to shoot. She was really superstitious." A tear ran down her cheek. She felt it fall onto her lips, tasted the saltiness of it. He wiped it away with his thumb and pulled her in against him, his arms around her.

"What was her favorite movie?" He asked quietly.

Deb sniffed. "Shall We Dance." He smiled.

"How about music? Who was on Kata's Playlist?"

Deb snuggled in against his chest. "Roy Orbison. She said 'Crying' was just about the sexiest thing she'd ever heard. Duran Duran. Anything from the 80s, really." She was quiet for a minute. "Gavin," she said after the pause. "Thanks."

"Hmmm. Sure. Always."

CHAPTER 33

As Gavin lay in the dark, Deb slept beside him, having cried herself to sleep. He felt terrible. She was dealing with her mother being murdered. How had it all become about him? He needed to reign it in. It seemed to be getting worse lately. He looked at his wrist to check the time, remembering he'd put his watch in the trash bag like a crazy person.

He slowly rose so as not to wake her. He slipped on his slippers and exited the bedroom. He headed out the front door and down the steps. He found the trash at the side of the house, next to the Hogue's property. He dug through the bags until he found the one with his bloodied clothing. He pulled it out and reached in, finding his watch at the bottom of the bag. He pulled it out of the bag, returning it to his wrist, and dropped the bag back in the trash can.

"I accidentally put my watch in the trash," he said to the woman behind him without turning around.

"Oh," Mrs. Hogue replied. "Was that blood?"

"Yes, Ma'am," he answered. "My girlfriend's mother was stabbed to death tonight. I tried to resuscitate her."

"That was the blonde's mother. I'm so sorry."

"Thank you," he said, turning to look at her.

She held out a can of Miller Lite. "Would you like a beer?"

He looked up at the dark windows of the house,

shrugged, and said, "Sure. Why not?"

He took the beer, cracked it open, and took a swig.

"Come on out to the patio," Mrs. Hogue invited. "Walt and I are just havin' a few beers and watchin' the night."

"Okay," he said, following her around the corner of her house. Her patio overlooked the river. They had fairy lights strung on the pergola. There was a cedar picnic table in the center of the concrete patio. He presumed it was Walt who sat at the picnic table with a beer and a bowl of chips in front of him.

"Walt," Mrs. Hogue said, confirming Gavin's presumption correct. "This is Detective...I'm sorry. I didn't get your name."

"Gavin Mahoney," he said, shaking the old man's hand.

Walt chuckled.

"Yeah, I know. But I promise, I'm half Irish."

"Irish Irish...or Boston Irish?" the old man laughed.

"Irish Irish. My father is from Dublin."

"My dad was in Ireland back in the '43. In the service. I ended up in Vietnam, myself."

"Afghanistan," Gavin said, raising his beer. The old man did the same. They drank.

"What branch?" he asked.

"Army."

"Hooah," Walt smiled. They drank again. "What division?"

"82nd Airborne," Gavin replied.

"You're Airborne! Me too. And my Dad. What rank, son?"

"First Lieutenant. You?"

Walt rose and stood at attention, saluting. Gavin saluted back. "At ease, soldier," he said with a smile.

Walt chuckled. "I was a private. My dad was a private. We were drafted. Have a seat, Lieutenant."

Gavin sat, and they drank a few beers together and talked for a while. The old man leaned forward and said, "Forgive my wife for earlier today, Lieutenant. A girl went missing from her home a few days ago. I know she came off a bit...racist...but she's not really. No more than most, anyway. She was freaked out by anybody rentin' that house this week."

"I don't hold grudges, Mr. Hogue."

Gavin looked around and pointed to the guitar case sitting by the door. "You play?"

"I do. You?"

Gavin nodded. "I didn't bring one, though."

"Betty Ann, go get that Yamaha," he said to his wife. She stood and went into the house, returning with a second case. She handed the case over to Gavin. He opened it and pulled out the instrument, admiring it. It was a nice guitar, not overly expensive, but well cared for.

Walt picked up his Martin out of the case Gavin had pointed out.

"So you know anything an old fart like me might know?"

Gavin smiled and tuned the guitar. Then he looked at the old guy and said, "How about a little Roy Orbison? 'Crying?'"

"I might know that one," the old man laughed.

Gavin said, "For Kathy Kaminski. You're loved." He started to play. Walt joined. Gavin sang. Walt harmonized.

Next door, the bedroom light came on. Moments later, Deb stood on the balcony, looking down on him as he sang. She disappeared back into the house as Dan and Miranda replaced her on the balcony. Gavin closed his eyes and finished the song, the notes still hanging in the air when he felt her hand lift his chin and her lips softly against his. He opened his eyes to look into the crystal blue eyes sparkling like gems under the fairy lights, looking back into his.

CHAPTER 34

Connie Davis was laying on the sofa in her reading nook on the second floor. She was snuggled up under a soft throw. It was a rainy evening and just a little cool. Her husband was working late at the office, and she was enjoying Shirley Jackson's *The Haunting of Hill House* again, with Carmen and Figaro, their two cats, and Buddy, Dan and Miranda's puppy. Carmen was lying on her back, draped across Connie's stomach. Figaro was perched on the arm of the sofa by Connie's head. Buddy was lying on her feet.

She was completely engrossed in the book. As the ghost was pounding on the doors, coming closer to the room where the girls were huddled together in terror, her heartbeat quickened. Then it was at the door. It was trying to break through.

Someone buzzed at the gate.

Connie screamed. She flung the book over the back of the sofa, where it flew over the banister and down to the floor at the foot of the stairs. Carmen flew in one direction, Figaro in the other. Buddy jumped off the sofa and barked. Connie jumped and clasped her chest. Then she started laughing.

She threw the throw off of herself and sat up, grabbing her phone off the coffee table in front of her. She checked the video feed at the gate. Oddly, no one was there. She shuddered slightly, thinking of her book. She rewound the video capture, catching two teenage boys pushing the buzzer and running away. She laughed again. *Great timing, boys! Good thing I was reading a real book and not on my tablet!*

She looked at the time. As if triggered by the late hour, her stomach rumbled. Sam had told her he'd be late and would be eating in Chicago. She hadn't bothered to cook, but she needed to get her book, anyway. She sighed, stretched, and stood up.

"Sorry, Guys," she crooned. "Ding dong ditchers. But let's go get something to eat."

She shoved her phone into her back pocket and headed down the stairs. Carmen, Figaro, and Buddy followed her. At the bottom of the stairs, she stooped and picked up her book. Carmen took the opportunity to shove her head under Connie's hand. "Yes, Carmen. I see you," she giggled, giving the cat a gentle pet before standing and making her way through the butler's pantry and into the kitchen. Buddy followed, wagging his tail.

As she flipped on the light, she had an overwhelming feeling of Mike. She'd had them more often since she'd put his pictures back up in the house, accepting grief instead of burying it. There was usually a reason for the feeling of his presence. What made her think of her son? She looked around. Nothing jumped out at her. Then she looked at the book in her hand. It wasn't her copy. It was Mike's. He'd written his name across the top on the cover. She laughed at herself. She'd been reading his copy all afternoon.

Mike was the reason she'd ever read the book, to begin with. He'd devoured books as a kid. This one was one of his favorites. His interests had been so eclectic. After he'd read this one three times, she'd decided to read it herself. It was completely outside of his normal taste. Hers, too. But the writing was compelling, and the story terrifying. She'd been unable to put it down. Sam was worried that it would give Mike nightmares. A valid concern, given he was only ten at the time, but Connie had shrugged it off. He'd already read the book three times and hadn't had any yet. And when he asked to watch the original 1963 horror classic, "The Haunting," based on the novel, she'd rented it and curled up beside him on the sofa with a big tub of popcorn. He'd dismissed the remake as garbage but loved that original version almost as much as the novel...almost.

"Ahhhhh. Mike, my boy," she sighed, hugging the book to her chest. "You'd have loved those ding dong ditchers for their timing." Her eyes teared up, but she welcomed the tears now. They meant time spent with her son.

She searched through the fridge and pulled out cheese and butter. She decided dinner would be Mike's favorite: grilled cheese sandwich and tomato soup.

After she'd prepared and eaten her dinner, sharing bits of cheese with the animals, and loaded her dishes into the dishwasher, her phone rang. She pulled it out of her pocket as she filled the pets' food and water bowls.

"Hey, Miranda! How's it going out in Virginia? - What? - Oh my God!"

CHAPTER 35

Connie watched and rewatched the video feed from the gate when Sam finally got home.

"What's going on, Love?" he asked, dropping his briefcase and pulling off his suit jacket. He hung the jacket over the back of the barstool.

Connie had opened the video on the television in the family room. She rewound the capture again. "I had a ding dong ditch at the gate this evening," she said, concentrating on the video.

"Okay? Did it scare you for some reason?"

"No. Well, yes, but only because I was at the part where the ghost is trying to get Eleanor."

He shook his head and laughed. "Why do you read that over and over?"

"Anyway," she interrupted sternly. "There are the boys in the middle of a downpour. Ding dong ditching our gate. Or so I thought." She paused the video capture of the two laughing faces. Their faces were obscured by the hoodies they had pulled over their heads, but the lower halves of their faces were clearly visible. "Who do they look like?"

Sam looked at the image. "I don't know."

"Mike and Dan."

He peered at the image again. "Maybe fifteen years ago."

She had a box from the attic at her feet. She reached in and pulled out a Batavia High School Hoodie, identical to the one the boy who resembled Mike was wearing in the video. "Mike's," she said, holding it up.

"Well, that's a coincidence, Honey."

She moved the hoodie around to the frayed sleeve, held it up, and pointed to the same fray on the video.

"What the…" Sam exclaimed.

"Somebody hacked our video feed and inserted an old video from fifteen years ago. Though where they got it, I couldn't possibly say. I mean, it's obviously from our system from back then. Look. Across the street at the door. That's Keith going into his house."

"Son of a…" he exclaimed, pulling out his phone and calling the sheriff directly.

While Sam talked to the sheriff, Connie dug deeper into the box. She found a research paper Mike had done on *The Haunting of Hill House* for his tenth-grade AP English class. She chuckled. *Now, that was a coincidence.*

She flipped through the pages. Halfway through the paper was a note from Mike. She looked closely at the staple. The original staple had been removed, and a new one had stapled the paper together again.

"Sam!" she called, flipping back to the note. She read out loud, "February 14, 2022. Dear Mom, Happy Birthday to me, huh? I can safely say there's nothing like a cancer diagnosis to ruin one's birthday. I'm keeping that to myself for a few days, though. I don't want to ruin it for Miranda. And I don't want to ruin Valentine's Day for you and Dad. Anyway, I figure, if I don't survive the leukemia or something else, you'd be the one to find this note. Know that I love you more than words can ever say. Tell Miranda she was right about Vanessa all along. But I'm right about Dan. I'm willing to bet he's divorced by the time you dig this out. I am keeping mad secrets, Mom. All about Dan. I have hidden a case file in the bottom of this box. It will explain a lot… but not everything. Love, Mike."

"Sheriff, I'm getting my gun out of the gun safe," Sam stated, running up the stairs.

He returned a moment later, carrying his weapon. Connie had pulled everything out of the box and had a case file in her hand.

"Who is that one for?" Sam asked. "Did Mike write a new will for Dan's maternal grandfather, too?"

"You're being facetious. But yes. Yes, he did," Connie replied.

"You're kidding? I thought he was Dominica's American Lit professor," Sam said, taking the folder.

"Benjamin Moore, II," Connie said, almost sounding amused.

Sam whistled. "You know any other partner's son would have bragged about bringing in such huge clients. Not mine. Mine hid the files. Let me guess: Dan inherits everything."

"Dan inherits everything."

The Sheriff buzzed at the gate. Sam let him in.

CHAPTER 36

Theodosia sat next to Miranda in the waiting area at the medical examiner's office in Manassas, Virginia. It was Sunday. Somehow, Sam Davis had arranged for them to get Kathy's body released despite it being the holiday weekend.

She turned and looked at the woman. "Your hair is really pretty. Is it natural?"

Miranda looked Theo in the eyes. "Um…yes."

"Oh. That's too bad. I mean, I was going to ask what color it is, but if it's natural, you wouldn't be able to tell me," Theo laughed.

"Auburn," Miranda replied with a smile.

"My hair is naturally just plain brown. I went blonde as soon as my mama let me, but honestly, everybody is blonde nowadays. How do you think I'd look with auburn hair?"

"Pretty as a picture," Miranda replied, putting her hand on Theo's arm.

"Wally's autopsy was performed in Richmond," the young widow announced. "Wally was not a nice man. He made money off getting people addicted to cigarettes and dying. And he didn't care one little bit. But he was nice to me. He liked the blonde." Her voice was tinged with a sadness Miranda had not noticed in her before.

"We're all more than one thing. Some of it's good; some bad," Miranda assured her.

"Nah, not like Wally. He was mostly bad. I know that. I'm not nearly as stupid as I seem."

"You're not stupid, Theo."

Theo grinned. "Thanks. I appreciate that. I'm still waiting for Wally's autopsy results. But I gave him a beautiful funeral. He was adopted, ya know. Can you imagine? Being adopted into all that old money? Didn't make him happy, though. He hated his parents."

"Wally was adopted? Really?"

"Sure. His birth mother was just a teenager when he was born. She went to some hospital in Minnesota where lots of unwed mothers went. He always said she abandoned him, and he hated her worse than the bitch who raised him, and that was sayin' somethin' 'cuz he really hated that bitch." Theo said.

"How old was Wally?"

"Sixty-five. He just turned sixty-five in April."

Dan, Gavin, Deb, and Frank emerged from the recesses of the medical examiner's office.

Dan smiled, "They're ready to release her body. We arranged for a nearby funeral home to prepare the body, and they'll fly her home tomorrow. Frank and Deb are going over to pick out a casket. I thought the rest of us could maybe get some lunch. The private plane is meeting us at Dulles. We can head home as soon as they get all the details ironed out."

Deb reached out, grabbed Gavin's hand, and gave him an imploring look. He gave it a squeeze and winked at her. "We'll go with you if you want. It's entirely up to you."

She nodded furiously and hugged him tightly.

Dan smiled, wrapping his arm around Miranda's shoulders as she stood up. "Or...we could all go to the funeral home and have lunch together after. Sorry. I believe I was a bit insensitive there."

Deb laughed. "It's okay. You're pragmatic. Sometimes, you can't see past that...right away. You usually catch on eventually, though."

He nodded. Miranda looked at him, puzzled. As the others exited the building, he kissed her cheek. "I'm not perfect, Baby. I had a huge hand in the demise of my marriage. Sometimes, I missed what she really needed from me. Please let me know when I do it to you. I'm sure I will. It's kind of a blind spot."

She stopped, wrapped her arms around him, and hugged him. "I love you, Danny. Warts and all. It's not like I'm so perfect, either. Actually, it's kind of nice to see some chinks in your armor." Then she laughed. "Oh my God, you're exactly like my father!"

"I'll take that! He's a great role model!" he smiled.

Frank laid his hand on Dan's shoulder. "I think you two are well suited for each other," he said with a grin.

"Ahhhhh! Jesus! Frank!" Dan jumped. "I forgot you were there!"

"Muhaha!" Frank said in his deepest voice.

Dan threw his head back and laughed. Miranda buried her face in Dan's chest, her shoulders shaking in laughter.

Her phone rang. She pulled it out of her back pocket. "Camille," she said, pulling out of Dan's embrace. She pushed the door open and walked through as she accepted the call.

"Hey, Camille! What's up?" she said as Dan and Frank followed her out. "Yeah, I actually just learned that a few minutes ago. Theo told me. Why is that important? – Who's Ivan?" She stopped and turned to look at Dan, shock registering on her face. "Oh, my God!"

She shook her head. "Danny, Honey. According to Ivan Polaski, who has been at Moore Robotics for 40 years, there were rumors that Walter Bowen may have been the illegitimate son of Ben Moore... the father of the current CEO. What?" She turned her attention back to Camille. "Mom found what? Noooooooo!" She grasped Dan's arm. "Mom found a case file Mike hid in the attic. He wrote a will for Ben Moore II. He's your mother's father. He's leaving everything to you!"

Much to her chagrin, Dan didn't look particularly surprised. "You knew!" she yelled, smacking him on his shoulder.

"I suspected," he laughed. He looked at the ground. "Kathy knew. I think it's what got her killed. She told me Jason and I are in danger. She handed me a cover letter from Mike to Benjamin Moore, II. It appeared to be the cover letter to a will. I think she found it on a boat in the yacht club called Dominica's Dream. It's registered to Ben Moore. He was an American Literature professor at U of I, Champaign, at the time Dominica was a student there. I remembered his being pictured in the yearbook."

"Okay? But did you know about Wally?" Theo asked, completely engrossed.

"I suspected," he repeated.

"How?" Deb asked.

Gavin blushed. Deb smacked his arm. "You knew!" Of course, *Gavin* knew, Miranda thought. Dan had been right about his being super smart.

"It's kind of our job, you know. Sara had a baby at Booth Memorial in April 1959. She was roommates with a 'Monica' who came from a wealthy family and had had an affair with an older married man. Monica was fifteen. Dominica would have been fifteen in 1959," he said sheepishly.

"Uncle Frank was born in 1960," Deb corrected him.

"Not me, Sweetheart. Booth Memorial wasn't that kind of hospital. In the '50s and '60s, it's where young girls went to give up their babies," Frank explained.

Dan nodded. "It's where Dominica got her friends to take her to have my mother in 1964."

"Oh. So, what you're saying is that there is another uncle out there." Deb said.

"Yes. But he's a perfectly nice man. Nothing at all like Victor. Maybe a bit...condescending and arrogant, but he's a good..." Gavin started.

Deb smacked his arm harder! "Noooooooo! Really? You can't be serious?"

"Oh my God!" Miranda exclaimed, smacking Dan's arm now, too.

Then, in unison, the two women incredulously exclaimed, "Special Agent Thomas Mathews?"

"Don't you two start that creepy crap," Dan said. Miranda smiled. She thought she saw Deb smile, too. The uncles were right. It was fun creeping Danny out. Gavin didn't even bat an eye. He was back to his stoney-faced self after his beautiful memorial to Kathy the other night.

"Wait. What? You're saying that FBI agent I talked to is Francie's brother?" Theo interrupted her thoughts. Theo looked around. "Darn it! I got nobody to smack!"

"Allow me, my dear," Frank said, offering his shoulder.

Theo backed away. "No offense, Cuz. I'm kinda afraid you might bite," she winked.

CHAPTER 37

Dr. Naomi Wise put on her reading glasses and looked at the "paper" on the computer in front of her. "How Tobacco Perverted Science to Sell and Profit Off Addiction and Death in African American Households." Not the most original of titles, but the student, a freshman in her Sociology Class at Howard University, certainly took a stance right from the opening. The girl had receipts.

She smiled. She liked the summer semesters. She saw some of the best work from students in these truncated semesters. She also liked working in her office on weekends. It wasn't unusual for her to be in her office on Sundays and holidays.

Dr. Wise was renowned in her field. She could teach anywhere. She chose Howard, her own alma mater. Howard University was as much a part of her self-identity as her own family. She'd been slightly disappointed when her granddaughter, Camille, had chosen Mary Washington University over Howard thirteen years prior, but the girl had been raised by her mother after all. Gwen Wise had never seen eye to eye with her learned mother-in-law. After Jameel had been killed in Afghanistan, Naomi had seen less and less of her granddaughter until the relationship was reduced to holiday telephone calls. Naomi sighed. She knew she was equally to blame, but it felt better to blame Gwen.

Uncertain as to why she was thinking of her granddaughter at that moment, she refocused on the paper in front of her. The student, Jameka Bradley, had included memorandums from Bowen Tobacco, dating decades back, all pushing the agenda to suppress scientific evidence about the addictiveness of nicotine. There was nothing new in them. This had all been exposed in several lawsuits over the last few decades, but this was an introductory sociology class, and Naomi was impressed with Jameka's thoroughness and resourcefulness.

One memo caught her attention and turned her focus back to her granddaughter. It mentioned a contract with Moore Robotics in Chicago. *Isn't that where Camille's husband is working?*

She opened her email and shot a quick note to Jameka. "I'm very impressed with your research. I'm curious about a memo you referenced dated September 1, 1998. Would you be available to review your source material this afternoon? I'd like to see the original memorandum."

Within minutes, Jameka had replied she'd be delighted and would be available at 12:30 pm.

Naomi penciled the girl in and called her granddaughter.

CHAPTER 38

Benjamin A. Moore, II despised his son, Benjamin A. Moore, III. It hadn't always been the case, though. He had loved him once, many years ago, when he was a child, but he had never really liked the man Benji grew into, and he'd grown to hate him over the last 68 years. He was well past giving a damn who knew it. He certainly didn't hide it from Benji.

Forty years ago, he'd backed a business venture Benji was interested in. It had been the only thing interesting the boy had ever brought to him. So, he had invested and allowed the boy to run the business. Moore Robotics had performed well. Benji had indeed built it into a multi-million-dollar venture. But he never could turn it over to his son. It all came back to the fact that he just couldn't stand him. He was amoral, egomaniacal, vain, and greedy. He was also really annoying. The sound of his voice grated on Ben's nerves.

It didn't help that Lilith had held the boy over him, keeping him married to that wretched shrew despite his undying love for Dominica until it was too late. Dominica's father had guaranteed she'd be stuck married to that little snivelly Geneli.

Ben had watched her cower in fear and regret for the rest of her life, and, fair or not, he blamed Benji. Had Benji never been born, Lilith would never have used him to keep Ben in line. He could have been happy. Dominica could have been happy.

But no. Lilith threatened to take the child. And he had loved the child. If only he'd foreseen how much like Lilith Benji would become, how much he'd hate him, he could have let her take him and not given a damn. But as his father always said, "There's no what if; there's only what is."

At 91, Ben was a grumpy old man, albeit a wealthy one, confined to a wheelchair and consumed with regret.

For the last twenty-five years, nearly twenty-six, he'd been looking for a way to destroy Benji. He'd seen the memo. His wretched offspring had conspired with Geneli, offering that...criminal...a contract for a factory that would bring him millions if Geneli could get rid of the girl and her child. The girl! She was the only good thing that had ever come from his love for Dominica. She had been his hope. When she and her child were killed less than two weeks later, he'd disowned Benji in his heart, though not legally. And as for that disgusting lump of humanity that Dominica's boy had become, he'd never even acknowledge him.

Dominica had sent Ben to the funny lawyer. She had a plan. He'd do anything for Dominica. She'd been right, and now Ben sat in his wheelchair daily, just waiting for the grandson to come destroy Benji and that wretched Walter Bowen, who he'd never acknowledge. Unfortunately, Walter went and died before it all came to fruition, but Walter's kid was just as odious. He'd do in a pinch. And if Ben could hang on long enough, he'd get to see it. If only Dominica had lived so long.

His nurse forced his pills into his mouth. He drank the water she put to his mouth. He'd take the pills without fighting her as he used to. The pills kept him alive. He wanted to live long enough to see it.

CHAPTER 39

Camille had texted Miranda that Naomi had called because a student had written a paper referencing a memo at Bowen Tobacco that mentioned Moore Robotics. Naomi would not let Dan or Gavin come to her meeting, stating that the police seemed like overkill, but she agreed Miranda could sit in and ask Jameka questions about the memo. So, the group delayed their departure and headed into DC and to Howard University once Deb and Frank had picked out a casket, the best the funeral home had available.

Miranda knocked gently on the door.

"Come in," Naomi called from inside her office.

Miranda opened the door and stuck her head in. "Uh, Dr. Wise? Hello?"

"Miranda! Dear! Come in." Naomi stood and walked around from behind her desk, opening her arms.

Miranda smiled and entered. She hugged her friend's grandmother. Naomi always intimidated Miranda just a little. She was a Pulitzer Prize winning author, an accomplished sociologist, a civil rights activist, and a legal expert. All of which she accomplished as a single teen mother, earning her doctorate before her son was out of middle school.

At 66, she was a young grandmother, having become a mother at fifteen. Jameel, Camille's father, had married Gwen right after graduation before he left for basic training.

Camille had been born when her parents were just twenty and nineteen. Naomi had become a grandmother at 35. Camille had an aunt two years her junior.

"You look great, Miranda. Love suits you."

"Oh, thank you, Dr. Wise," she blushed.

"So, why's it so important you see this memo?" Naomi asked, returning to her seat behind her desk.

"Well, it's a long story, Dr. Wise, but I'll make it as quick as possible. My fiancé, Dan...well, his mother and sister were murdered when he was five, in September 1998. His mother had been adopted. Her biological mother turned out to be a very wealthy Chicago socialite named Dominica Geneli. Dominica had an affair with her American Literature Professor, Benjamin Moore, II, at U of I. Her husband, whom her father forced her to marry after she'd had Dan's mom, wanted his sons to inherit Dominica's fortune, but she kept Dan a secret and left everything to him. When Dominica passed away in October, they learned of Dan's existence. They went on a crime spree that included breaking into my parents' house and assaulting me. But in the end, Dan caught them. But now we've learned Dan's mother was the second child that she had with Ben Moore. The first being Wally... Walter Bowen, when she was just fifteen."

"Well, I can relate to that," Naomi smiled.

"Yes, Ma'am," Miranda smiled back.

"Anyway, it turns out Ben Moore also changed his will to leave everything to Dan. And now, Kris, who raped me in college and happens to be Walter's son, has shown up, kidnapped Jason, Dan's son, threatened Pete with a gun, put him in an explosive vest and threatened everyone at Moore Robotics, and has begun stalking me. He probably killed Dan's ex-wife's mother. That memo might connect Walter to the Genelis and the murder of Dan's mother and sister."

"Wow. That's a lot to unpack."

"It's the really condensed version. But yeah, it sounds really crazy. And I didn't even go into the circus performers, armored truck robbery, and vampires." Miranda burst into nervous laughter.

"Circus…" Naomi laughed. "Okay, I'll let you talk to Miss Frost. She's agreed to allow you in our meeting already, but maybe keep that whole story to yourself, okay?" She sat back and folded her hands together thoughtfully, looking perplexed.

Miranda brightened, an idea occurring to her. She pulled out her phone and opened several articles printed in the Chicago Tribune, reporting on the events starting in late October through Christmas. She then texted the links to Naomi, who looked at them with a raised eyebrow.

At precisely 12:30 pm, Jameka knocked on the door of the office. She was a tall, thin girl, pretty, stylish. She was not what Miranda had pictured in her head. Knowing Naomi had praised the girl's work, Miranda had expected a bookish student. Jameka had the poise and presence of a beauty queen. An observation that was dead on accurate, as it turned out. Jameka had been Miss Teen Maryland and one of the top ten Miss Teen America contestants in 2023. She was making use of the scholarships she had won.

"I have a hard copy of the memo you asked about, Dr. Wise. I referenced the part applicable to the theme in my paper. The rest is just…well, gibberish, as far as I can tell. It talks about a girl and her child standing in the way and Geneli Architecture being awarded the contract to design an e-cigarette factory in Henrico County if they could rectify the situation. I assume someone was a standout on the land sale, but it didn't apply to my paper. I'm afraid I didn't dig any deeper."

Naomi nodded. "Jameka, your paper is outstanding, but you missed something very important by narrowing your focus. I'm not counting that against your grade, but you show a great deal of promise, so I hope you take the note."

"What did I miss?" she asked, clearly perplexed.

Miranda took the memo into her hands and read it. "A contract for murder," she replied excitedly. "May I take a picture of this document?"

"Uh, sure," Jameka replied. "A contract killing? Really? I had no idea. I mean, other than the thousands who die from lung cancer and emphysema each year."

Miranda took a picture with her phone.

"Jameka, I'd love to keep you updated. Can I have your number?" Miranda asked with a smile.

"Sure."

Miranda handed her the phone and she added herself to the contacts.

"Please let me know what happens as well, Miranda. I love a good noir novella," Naomi needled. "Circus performers! Ha!"

"I will, Dr. Wise. I hope you'll be at the wedding."

"Honestly, I was going to decline the invitation, but I've just changed my mind. I'll be there," she smiled.

"Oh! Awesome. We'll see you next month then! Please excuse me. We need to get back to Chicago. Thank you both for your help." Miranda blushed and rose from her seat, backing into the door as she spoke. She found the doorknob to make a hasty exit. God, why did that woman make her so nervous.

CHAPTER 40

Dan hired a group of students from the criminology department at Howard to deliver the Escalades back to Ava's. There were three of them, two to drive the Escalades and one to follow in his car and bring all three back to Howard. He paid each $500 and gave the one with his own vehicle an extra $100 for the return trip. Dan programmed the address in the GPSs. The kids were massively excited not only for the extra money but also to drive the Escalades.

Then he called for a limo to take them to Dulles.

As they waited, Dan looked at the image of the memo. It was in house at Bowen Tobacco, between Walter Bowen and the CFO, his brother-in-law, Nathan Guthrie. Nathan was married to Walter's adopted sister, Martha. Martha had been adopted as an infant by the Bowens when Walter had turned five, and, as he did the rest of the family, he treated her with disdain. But as she grew, he had oddly bonded with her. When she and Nathan died in a car accident in 2007, he took in her children, in a sense. He sent them to a property in New Orleans and emptied their trust funds "for the cost of their care." Of course, none of this was in the memo. Dan researched the details as he read.

"What do you know? Cain and Amber Guthrie are Walter's adopted sister's kids. Looks like he pretty much robbed their trust funds dry and left them destitute when they turned eighteen. To make up for it, he hired Cain, AKA Caleb, as a chauffeur and Amber as a clerk at the New Orleans Plantation the family owns."

"You're kiddin'? That kid was 'is nephew?" Theo asked. "Wow. He treated him like any other regular chauffeur. Worse even, sometimes."

Dan nodded. "Yeah, Theo, Wally was a piece of crap. Sorry."

She blinked. "Yeah, I know."

"Anyway, the memo is from Wally to Nathan, the CFO at the time, Caleb and Amber's father. Jameka was only interested in the first paragraph where Wally dismisses the most recent study, advising that was for cigarettes, not e-cigarettes... and wow...that they need to lower the price of the e-cigarette device, as it won't appeal to African Americans, while raising the price of regular cigarettes to offset the difference. Quote: 'One way or the other, they'll buy our products.'" He shook his head.

"I told ya, he was not a good man," Theo acknowledged.

"Here's what pertains to my situation: 'I have learned from S. Geneli that his wife's daughter has been located and that she has a child. B. Moore brokered deal with Geneli Architecture to design Henrico County factory. Will give Geneli contract if he can arrange for that situation with the Bradley woman to be rectified as we have previously discussed.'"

He looked up, fighting back the tears in his eyes. "It's vague. It's hardly damning. But it seems clear to me. Salvatore colluded with Walter Bowen to kill my mother." He wiped his eyes. "I'll get Judy to dig through Geneli's records. Hopefully, Salvatore and Geno didn't destroy them. And, of course, Art might know something."

Gavin spoke as he looked at the ground. "And Salvatore

and Geno will know, too. And…"

"And…what?" Dan asked. Gavin, he had begun to understand, only doled out information in small, need-to-know nuggets. Gavin turned his gaze to Deb. She looked back at him as if she were trying to read his thoughts. Good luck with that, Dan thought.

But then Deb gasped, "The Christmas decorations!"

"What?" Dan asked. Gavin broke his gaze and nodded. Holy crap! Deb did read his thoughts. Miranda was always saying that Dan was an open book. Gavin was a locked book. But not just locked…a wrapped tightly in a chain, padlocked, put in a safe, sealed in concrete, and dropped in the ocean locked. But Deb had never once read *Dan's* thoughts.

"After you moved out that Christmas Eve, Mom put her Christmas decorations in my attic. There was a box of old files in there, too. I didn't pay any attention to them. I was looking for Christmas decorations, not files, but some were Geneli files. After you told me she had worked there, I didn't give it any thought. Oh, my God. What if I've had it all along?"

"I admit, I never looked through them either. I should have. Kathy always had a purpose for everything she did. Damn. I feel foolish," Gavin blushed. "Kathy had blackmail material on good ole Sal."

"How exactly do you know about the Christmas decorations?" Dan asked, chuckling. Seriously, how had it taken these two 6 months to get into bed?

"Oh, I helped take them down."

"So. She lied? Do you think she knew exactly who Kris Bowen was?" Dan asked. Gavin shrugged. "If you had what I need, Kathy, I'll owe you big time!" Dan said, looking skyward.

Frank shook his head. "Don't admit you owe anything to the dead."

"Seriously," agreed Theo.

CHAPTER 41

Special Agent Thomas Mathews sat looking at the private jet waiting on the tarmac. Finally, the limo arrived. The four who had flown into Virginia on that jet had added two to their party. The man was bald, but it looked to be a fashion choice, as his head was shaved, and the stubble appeared to cover his head. He was shorter than Tom but still similar in build. He was also incredibly pale. He could be anywhere between forty years old and seventy. It was impossible to tell. The girl was bleached blond, buxom. Her clothes were expensive but tacky. "Hmmm. Guess the Widow Bowen and her weird cousin are joining us in Chicago," he mused to the agent beside him in the driver's seat. "I'll see you in Chicago, Agent Belcher."

The agent smiled and waved as Tom exited the vehicle. "See ya. Enjoy the private jet."

Tom strode across the tarmac toward the group. The ex-wife paused for some reason as he approached. She looked like she was about to cry as she gazed at him. He slowed his pace, puzzling over the reaction. *Her mother was murdered. There's nothing out of the ordinary about her crying.* His pace quickened again, and he joined them.

"Good afternoon," he said.

Inexplicably, the ex-wife rushed him, hugging him and kissing his cheek.

"What's happening?" he asked.

The trooper with the Irish name and Mexican face blushed. "Uh, I haven't told him, Deb. He doesn't know." Tom wondered what he was talking about.

She blushed in turn and laughed, releasing Tom from her embrace. "Come aboard, Uncle Tom. We've got a lot to tell you." *Uncle?*

The pale, bald man chuckled.

"Uncle? Ma'am, I'm sorry for your loss, but I think you're suffering some kind of mental break," he said, following her up the stairs and onto the plane.

She sat down and motioned for him to sit across from her. Then, the trooper sat beside her. The bald, pale guy sat directly across the aisle, and the widow sat next to him. The deputy and the fiancé moved as far forward as they could. *What the hell?*

"We're all aboard, Max," the deputy said to the pilot over an intercom.

"Thank you, Mr. Bradley. We'll be ready to take off in a few minutes."

Tom took the seat indicated by the ex-wife. They all buckled in.

Once they were situated, a stewardess appeared from the cockpit and asked if they wanted any drinks.

"No, thanks," Tom answered.

"Agent Mathews, you're going to want a drink," interrupted the bald, pale man.

Tom looked around. The trooper nodded.

"Um. Okay. Whiskey. Whatever you got."

"Neat, or on the rocks?" the stewardess asked with a smile.

"Neat," he replied.

She poured a shot of Johnny Walker Blue. He held up his hand. "Uh, make it a double."

She smiled again and poured out the double.

The others all ordered. She served them and disappeared.

"Okay? What's with the Addams Family treatment?" Tom asked.

The trooper cleared his throat. "A few days ago, I followed up with Kathy Kaminski's elderly mother regarding something Kathy told Tim, the trooper who spoke to her after Jason was kidnapped."

"What? Nobody said anything about her mother," Tom replied, his dander rising.

"Nobody thought it meant anything. But I'd come to know Kathy. She rarely said or did anything without a purpose. Granted, she was delusional, so it was a crapshoot. I decided to follow up anyway. She told Tim to ask her mother about Monica. So, I did. Monica was Sara's, Kathy's mother's, roommate at Booth Memorial in April 1959. Sara was seventeen. Monica…Dominica was fifteen. They both had boys. Dominica's son was adopted by Boyd and Edith Bowen, an adoption prearranged by Dominic Ricardi. Sara's was adopted by Quinton and Elizabeth Mathews."

"The hell you say!" Tom exclaimed.

The ex-wife smiled sweetly and opened her arms. "Welcome to the family, Uncle Tom!"

Tom looked at the pale, bald man. He suddenly realized that his facial features bore more than a passing resemblance to his own.

He downed his double. "Deputy Bradley! Can I get another?" he called.

The fiancé's phone beeped. She took it out and read the incoming text. Her eyes grew hugely wide, her mouth went slack, dropping open. She appeared unable to speak.

She replied to the text and handed the phone off to the

deputy, who, upon reading it, went ashen and called the pilot over the intercom, asking him to delay take-off because there would be another passenger.

The stewardess reappeared with the expensive whiskey. "Leave the bottle," the Deputy said, holding out his glass to Tom, who had taken it and poured out his second drink.

CHAPTER 42

Jameka Bradley took Dr. Wise's criticism: Don't narrow your focus too much. She didn't know what the professor's friend was looking for or how she'd arrived at the conclusion she'd reached, but she looked long and hard at the memo. And then she shoved it into her folder and headed to the library.

The friend had been from Chicago, so she started with the *Chicago Tribune*. She began with September 1, 1998, and searched through each paper, looking for any of the names mentioned in the memo. She found very little. She sighed heavily and was about to put away the papers when an article caught her eye: Moore Robotics, LLC, a subsidiary of Moore Industries, would be sponsoring a job fair at Northland Mall in Sterling, IL, seeking entry-level robotic engineers on September 10, 1998.

September 10, 1998.

The date was like a neon sign flashing in her brain. *Dad?*

Jameka's mother was a proud African American woman. Her father was a white man, a truck driver Angelica Frost had met in a dive bar in La Plata, Maryland, nearly twenty years ago. He was on a long haul. According to her mother, they were just two lonely people who found comfort with each other. They never intended to be more to each other than what they were in a dark barroom one night. When her mother got pregnant, he offered her whatever support she wanted. He took care of Jameka. He provided for her, but her parents were never together. He wasn't a part of her daily life.

Several years back, he'd gotten married and moved to a town just across the river. He'd made more of an effort to be a part of her life. She'd grown close to him over the last 4 years of his life. He'd died a year ago now.

He'd confided on his deathbed that he had a son, whom he had adopted after marrying the boy's mother, that he'd hoped to introduce him to her. He then told her the story of his wife and daughter.

She pulled the memo out again. "I have learned from S. Geneli and B. Moore that his wife's daughter has been located and that she has a child. B. Moore brokered a deal with Geneli Architecture to design Henrico County factory. Will give Geneli contract if he can arrange for that situation with the Bradley woman to be rectified as we have previously discussed," she read.

She had little to connect the memo to her father or the tragic story he told her, but she literally had chills. She shivered and rubbed her arms.

"What did Dad say? Stay away from...Bowen Tobacco...not cigarettes... Bowen. He said, 'Bowen will kill you.' Damn. I didn't narrow my focus enough."

She had added that woman Miranda Davis's number to her contacts after Miranda left Dr. Wise's office, getting the number from Dr. Wise. She pulled out her phone and texted, "My father was a man named Keith Bradley. His wife and baby daughter were murdered in 1998 in a small town in Illinois. He has a surviving son I've never met. I don't know why, but I got chills looking at the Tribune dated 9/10/98 with an article about Moore Robotics. Please tell me this memo isn't about that!"

Miranda texted back almost immediately, "OMG!"

A few minutes passed. Miranda texted again. "We're waiting on the tarmac at Dulles. Agent Belcher of the FBI will pick you up at your dorm room in ten minutes. He'll bring you here. You are not safe."

She followed it with a picture of a man and the warning: "This man will hurt you! If you see him, RUN!"

It was a picture of Kris Bowen, son of Walter Bowen, the heir apparent to the CEO position at Bowen Tobacco. *What the hell?*

Jameka was confused. Agent Belcher was waiting at her dorm when she made it back. He advised her to pack a bag and get her research. She had no intention of going anywhere and told him so.

"Please, Miss Bradley. It's for your own safety. Kris Bowen is a dangerous fugitive."

"I don't see why that puts me in any danger!" she insisted.

The agent looked nervously out her window.

"We don't have time to argue. We have to go. Now." He pointed out across the campus.

There he was. He was holding a map and clearly looking for a building. It was the evil in his eyes that convinced her.

"What about my things?" she asked, panicked.

"No time!" the agent replied, taking her arm and rushing her out of her building to his car he'd parked just outside.

"Can you tell me where I'm going?"

"No, Ma'am. My job is to get you to a plane waiting on the tarmac at Dulles. You'll find out the rest when you get there."

She noticed he looked back a lot, but his expression revealed nothing. *Was that the same car she'd seen when they'd peeled away from Howard? No! It couldn't be.*

"Are we being followed?" she asked, fear filling her voice.

"Don't worry. I'll get you there safely," he replied. He almost smiled.

Within minutes, besides his calm demeanor, she began to doubt there had been any danger at all. She looked at him with a side-eye. "You playin' me, Agent Belcher?"

"No, Ma'am. I am not."

She sat quietly for the rest of the ride, and at the end of thirty minutes, she found herself exiting the car and staring at a private jet.

Miranda Davis emerged from the plane. She jogged over to Jameka, hugged the girl, and led her to the plane. Jameka climbed the stairs and entered. Miranda followed her on board. The door closed. A handsome man of about thirty stood just inside the plane's cabin. He had curly brown hair, a great jawline, and the most amazing green eyes Jameka had ever seen.

"Hello, Jameka. I'm Dan Bradley," he said.

"You're Dan? How? I don't understand," Jameka said.

"Neither do I," he replied. He motioned for her to sit down. He buzzed the pilot on the intercom. "Our last passenger is aboard. Whenever you're ready."

Miranda's phone rang. She jumped. She looked at it and nearly dropped it. Dan steadied her hand. "It's okay. Answer it. On speaker," he said calmly.

"Hello, Kris," she stammered. She bit her thumbnail.

"Hello, Miranda. Hello, Cousin. Guess ya got ta ya sista first. Pity. She's a pretty girl. I'd've enjoyed her company," said the voice over the phone.

"I beg your pardon! Who do you think you are?" Jameka yelled, more angry than scared in the moment.

Kris just laughed and hung up.

Jameka looked around at the odd group of people.

"Hello, I'm Special Agent Tom Mathews. I just learned that this is my niece Deb, my brother Frank, and…Uhhhhhh, cousin's daughter, I guess…Theo, the widow Bowen. Oh, and Deb's boyfriend, Gavin."

"Good job using our names, Uncle Tom," the woman he'd introduced as Deb giggled nervously.

"Just learned?" Jameka asked, taking a seat.

"Uh. Yes. I was adopted as a baby. I always knew that. Turns out this assignment brought me into contact with my birth family."

"Wow. Quite the night for family reunions on this plane, huh?" Jameka pondered.

Dan sat down beside her, and Miranda beside him. The pilot announced takeoff, and they began to taxi.

As soon as they were airborne, Dan, who was sitting silently, staring at his feet, sighed deeply and buried his face in his hands. "I just don't understand. Why? Why would he not tell me?"

Miranda rubbed his back. He grabbed her and pulled her to him. He openly cried.

Jameka sat there, feeling awkward as hell.

Deb leaned across the aisle and patted her knee. "It isn't you, Honey. It's that he and his dad were really close, and he just can't wrap his head around why he kept you a secret."

"Oh, I understand. It's not too much fun being a big secret, either," Jameka replied.

Dan wiped his eyes. "I'm sorry, Jameka. Really, I am. You're right. This is hard on you, too. You must be confused and scared and…"

"Angry," she finished.

He nodded, swallowing hard. "Hold on. Maybe someone can answer some of our questions." He picked up the plane's phone, dialed a number, and put it on the plane's speaker. It rang twice.

"Hello?" came the woman's voice.

"Ava," he said, his voice cracking.

"Hey, Honey! Where are ya callin' from?" the woman asked.

"Ava. Tell me about Jameka. Keeping in mind, she's sitting right here."

There was a long silence. "Hello, Jameka," the woman said, her voice catching. "I'm your stepmother, Ava Bradley. But I guess you know that already."

"Ava!" Dan said sternly.

"I know, Doll. I know. I shoulda told ya. Hell...HE shoulda told ya!" Ava replied. "I don't know what to tell ya. Angelica asked him to be a 'silent partner,' so to speak. It was just a one-night thing. He respected her wishes. He didn't think it was fair to tell you about a baby sister you'd never get to be a brother to. He only really got to spend any time with Jameka over the last four years of his life because she'd asked her mother about him. He wanted you two to meet, but Angelica was wary. I can't blame her for that. She didn't really know your father, Dan. She raised Jameka on her own. He let her call the shots. As for me, I just didn't know what to do. I'm glad you're together now. I watched your pageant on TV, Jameka. I DVR'd it. He'd have been so proud. He was so proud. Of both of you."

CHAPTER 43

Angelica Frost was standing in the checkout line at Food Lion. With Jameka away at Howard University, she had grown accustomed to buying small amounts of groceries daily instead of the weekly shopping she'd done when Jameka was home. Tonight, she planned on a simple chicken cutlet, brown rice, and a baby spinach salad, a low-fat, nutritious meal. Having a beauty queen for a daughter had inspired her to learn the proper way to eat and maintain her figure, which was still quite good at fifty-six.

She paid for her groceries, and her phone rang. She didn't recognize the number. She answered. "Hello?"

"Hey, Ma."

"Jameka?" She looked at the phone number again. "Where are you?"

"On a private jet owned by my brother, Dan, on my way to Chicago."

"You're where?" her mother yelled. "Jameka! You don't know that man! You don't know he's your brother!"

"He didn't know I existed, Ma."

"What?"

"Dad's wife said you told Dad that you didn't want him in my life!"

"Jameka! Come on. Why would I..." she started.

"Exactly. Why would you? You knew I wanted to

know my family, Ma."

"I'm your family!" Angelica interrupted angrily.

"And you always will be. So why did you ask Dad not to let me meet my brother?"

"He's NOT your brother! Your dad adopted him. He's not blood."

"Really, Ma?" Jameka was crying.

"Your dad was afraid for that boy. Afraid people would be comin' after him. I didn't want those people comin' after you!" Angelica explained.

"Too late, Ma. They already did. That's how I ended up here."

"Ms. Frost," said an unfamiliar masculine voice. "This is Dan. I need you to get on a plane to Chicago. Please. My fiancé, Miranda, will send you a ticket. Please. I don't know if you're safe. Don't go home. We'll get you anything you need here. Please."

"What? I can't."

"Ms. Frost. This is Special Agent Tom Mathews, FBI. I highly recommend you come to Chicago," said a second, older voice.

"Okay. I'll do it."

The call disconnected. And within seconds, a ticket leaving BWI in 3 hours had been sent to her phone. She didn't trust these people. And she wasn't leaving her daughter with them. She dropped her groceries in a trash can and got into her car, driving directly to BWI.

CHAPTER 44

Connie unlocked the front door, shuffling through the stack of mail in her hand. She flipped on the lights inside the entrance to her house, kicked the door shut with her knee, and reset the alarm system.

She pulled a manilla, bubble-lined envelope from the stack of mail. She furrowed her brow. It was addressed to her. The return address read only, "Mike." The postal mark was Colonial Beach, Virginia, but the handwriting was not Miranda's or Dan's, and it certainly wasn't Mike's. The penmanship was feminine: neat, curly.

She tore the envelope open and dumped two small DVDs on the console table inside the front door, the kind from an old DVD video camera. She picked them up and headed upstairs to Mike's old bedroom. He had an old laptop. In there with a disc drive.

Oddly, she found it fully charged, though not plugged in. Sam must have charged it for some reason. She booted it up and inserted the first disc into the drive.

The list of videos appeared on the screen. There were only two. She clicked the first. It was the video feed she'd seen last evening. The one that someone had inserted, showing the ding dong ditch.

She clicked the second. Like the first, it was a video from fifteen years prior. It showed Miranda in the driver's seat of Connie's old Mercedes. Connie was in the passenger seat. She smiled at the memory. She'd been teaching Miranda to drive. Suddenly, Dan ran into view and up to Miranda. There was no sound, but he appeared to speak to her. Then he laughed and leaned in and kissed her cheek through the car window. Connie laughed at the video. Miranda blushed. Dan ran off, and Miranda pulled forward through the open gate.

Connie gasped and paused the video. There, across the street. A Bently was parked outside the Bradley house. A man got out of the driver's seat. He was elderly. He walked with a cane. He stood and watched either Miranda and Connie or Dan for a minute. She couldn't be sure which. There was a woman in the passenger seat of the car. She lowered her window and spoke to the man. Dominica Geneli. Connie was positive it was her. Then the man got back into his car and drove away. His vanity plate read "Moore."

Connie removed the disc from the drive. She inserted the second. There was only one file. The video was of a man, no one she recognized. He entered an office. He looked around. He went to a computer and inserted a disc like the ones she had just received. He sat behind the desk, typed on the keyboard, removed the disc, shoving it into his pocket. He shut off the computer. She didn't understand what she was looking at. She looked closely at the desk. The flip calendar showed September 1, 19… She zoomed in…1998. The nameplate read Benjamin A. Moore, III.

She didn't believe that man was Benjamin Moore, III. He looked nothing like the elderly man in the other video. His clothes were cheap, ill-fitting. He was overweight. He needed a haircut. Nothing about his appearance screamed money. Nothing.

She put the discs back in the envelope and shut off the computer. She grabbed the envelope and left the room, closing the door behind her.

CHAPTER 45

The Honda Civic pulled into the driveway of the small gray ranch on E 26th Street, just four houses from the dead end into a field. Brandon Kaminski opened the front door and waved. It had turned out that Katelynn's father was not Roger Kaminski, as her birth certificate had proclaimed, but Brandon didn't care. She was still a sister to him. He'd grown up an only child in an extended family where he was the only only child. He relished having two beautiful sisters, and since having met them over New Year's Day, he'd doted on them.

Katelynn was barely an inch taller than his eldest daughter, Kelly. She was as cute as a bug. He ran out in his bare feet to hug the girl. She'd just lost her mother, and he wanted to show as much love and support as he could...

Brandon was a big man with a big personality. His tiptoeing across his front lawn in his bare feet with his outstretched like a ballerina would embarrass his daughters and doubtless make his "sister" laugh. So that's what he did. Katelynn immediately cracked up and rushed to him. He grabbed her up like a rag doll, hugging her and swinging her.

"Hey, Marlon Brando," she quipped as he lowered her back to the ground. The nickname had come into being immediately when he'd quoted the Godfather incessantly at their first meeting."I'm so sorry about your mom. Are you hungry? You want something to eat before you head into the

'Burbs?"

"No. I gotta get Jason and meet Deb. She said it's important. I ate before I left Moline, anyway."

She looked around and leaned toward her giant brother. "Um, is Uncle Bob around?"

Brandon shrugged. "Somewhere."

"Deb wants you to meet her at Mr. and Mrs. Davis's house, Uncle Bob! She says it's important!" she called to the neighborhood. "Not that he won't follow me anyway," she added in a quieter tone.

"Aunt Tatie!" Jason exclaimed, running from the house and jumping into his young aunt's arms.

Brandon moved Jason's car seat from his SUV to the backseat of Katelynn's Honda Civic.

She buckled him into it. Melissa, Brandon's wife, had emerged from the house with Jason's things. She handed them over to Katelynn.

As quickly as she'd arrived, she was gone again.

CHAPTER 46

Angelica made her way to baggage claim, though she had none to claim. As she came down the escalator, she saw the uniformed chauffeur holding the sign with her name on it. She shook her head.

The ticket they'd sent to her phone had been first class. She'd never flown first class before. Jameka had said she was aboard a private jet. She'd certainly never been on a private jet before. She had ridden in a limo, of course, but she'd never had one waiting for her at baggage claim, with a driver who was better dressed than she. Keith was a truck driver! Where the hell did all this money come from? Had her Baby-Daddy played her for fourteen years? Should she have been asking and getting a lot more child support?

She approached the driver. "I'm Angelica Frost," she stated.

"Yes, Ma'am. I was told you do not have any luggage. If that's incorrect..."

"I don't have any luggage. I'm chasin' down my crazy daughter," she said, waving her hand at him.

"Of course, then right this way, Ms. Frost." He led the way to a large limo at the curb.

"The limo is fully stocked. Help yourself to anything you'd like. I'm afraid Mr. Bradley only arranged for one limo, so you'll be sharing the ride. Mrs. Bradley is already inside, waiting for us."

"Mrs. Bradley? He married?" she asked.

"No, Ma'am. He is engaged. This Mrs. Bradley is his stepmother." He opened the door.

She paused, her breath seemingly taken away by the announcement of with whom she was sharing her ride. She smiled nervously. The chauffeur was a young man of color, even though he was ever so proper. Surely, he'd understand.

"Uh. Well, I guess we'll try to keep Jerry Springer out of this. But you're about to give me a ride with my Baby-Daddy's wife."

He grinned, and she saw she'd read him correctly, all the proper melting away and the swag seepin' through. Then it was gone. The proper taking over again.

She climbed in.

Ava looked up and smiled, holding out a flute of champagne, "Angelica Frost! It's so nice to finally meet you! I'm Ava Bradley."

"Well, hey, Mrs. Bradley. Nice to meet ya, too," Angelica replied, taking the glass.

"Just how much money does this man got?" She looked around at the opulence.

"More than God," sighed Ava.

Despite herself, Angelica burst into laughter.

"No, I'm serious. Even as we speak, he's having two brand-new Escalades dropped off at my house. You want one?"

"What? Nah. I need tuition money for Jameka, not a fancy SUV," she laughed.

Ava shook her head no.

"Whatchu mean no?" Angelica laughed.

"That he already paid that for next year. Seriously. Red or Silver?"

Angelica just sat there with her mouth open. "He don't even know Jameka," she stammered when she found her voice.

"No. But he knows that she's his father's daughter. That's all he needs to know." Ava patted Angelica's knee. "Let me tell you about Dan Bradley."

CHAPTER 47

Sam came home to find his wife once again frantically cooking. Fried chicken. At least 4 whole birds. Mashed potatoes. Gravy. Biscuits. Green beans.

"What army are we feeding?" he asked with a laugh.

"Everybody. I'm not sure this is even enough."

"Everybody? On Earth?"

"Might as well be. Pete, Camille, Liam, Annalise, Deb, Gavin, Jason, Katelynn, Bob, Frank, Theo Bowen, Agent Mathews, Dan, Miranda, Ava, Angelica Frost, and Jameka."

"Okay, I don't know those last two," he quipped, digging a finger into the mashed potatoes and then popping it into his mouth. He loved her cooking. She smacked his hand and rolled her eyes.

"Oh, Sam! It's too good," she grinned. "Jameka is Keith's daughter. And Angelica is her mother."

He stood there with his finger still in his mouth, unmoving, not even blinking.

"But there's more."

"More than that bombshell? Can my heart handle it?" he asked, laughing at his wife's enthusiastic gossiping.

Connie leaned in. "Agent Mathews is Frank, Bob, and Kathy's biological brother." She giggled and covered her mouth with her hand.

"I knew it!'

"Oh, you did not."

"Okay, I didn't. But I knew he reminded me of someone."

"And on a darker note, Walter Bowen was the biological son of Ben Moore and Dominica. Kris Bowen is Dan's cousin," she added with a frown.

Someone buzzed the gate. Sam looked at his phone and opened it for Pete and Camille.

"How much do you think Mike knew? I can't believe he hid these things so effectively."

She audibly gasped. He looked at her with a puzzled expression. She pointed at the envelope she'd laid on the table. Sam picked it up. "Mike? Who'd do such a thing?"

"Mike would," she replied.

He looked at her, worried.

"Oh, I know that isn't Mike's handwriting! He didn't physically send me those DVDs. They're very interesting, by the way. They're obviously very important. I just don't understand how. My first guess is Ava, given the postmark, but that doesn't really make sense. Then I remembered Mary Cummings was originally from Colonial Beach. You'd hired her based on a recommendation from Ava. Didn't you tell me she moved home after she resigned a few months ago?"

"Why would my former executive assistant mail you DVDs from Mike?" he asked, as the Camachos exited their minivan, and the twins came bounding across the patio toward the kitchen door on the other side of the bay window. He moved to the door, opening it, and letting the family in, resetting the alarm.

"Because he'd asked her to, of course."

"Before he died, he asked her to send you DVDs over a year and a half after he died?" He looked at the handwriting again. "It does look like her writing, though." It sounded absolutely absurd. But so did this whole convoluted mess.

Pete asked, "Those the DVDs you wanted me to check out, Mrs. Davis? I brought my equipment like you asked."

"Yes, Thank you, Pete. Sam, go help Pete," she said, shooing them out of her kitchen and returning her attention to the chicken.

CHAPTER 48

Gavin followed Deb into her house. She made her way to her hallway and reached up, pulling down the door to the attic. "They're just to the right. The file box should be behind them. I kind of pushed it back because it didn't have any Christmas ornaments in it. Watch out for spiders," she said, waving for Gavin to go up the ladder.

Instead of climbing the ladder, he grabbed her around the waist and pulled her in, kissing her, taking her breath away, as well as his own.

"Later," she whispered, tapping his chest with her hand, her mouth still just brushing his.

"Uh-huh. Later," he whispered back, pulling her back in and kissing her again. Her legs trembled, and he smiled. "Hmmm. Good to know."

"What's good to know?"

"That I have the same effect on you that you do on me."

"Oh."

Bob cleared his throat. He was standing just inside Jason's bedroom door, looking at them through the ladder rungs.

Gavin let go of Deb. "What's scary is I'm getting used to that," he said, nodding toward Bob and climbing the ladder.

Bob chuckled.

"Thanks, Uncle Bob," Deb sighed. "You're going to scare him off!"

"This one? Never. He's here to stay," Gavin heard him say, as he searched through the boxes. Where had he seen it at Christmas?

"Got it! Ahhhhh. Big spider!" Gavin called from the attic. "Here, Bob, take this box." He handed the file box down to Deb's uncle.

"See. Spiders make him flinch. Not quirky uncles," Bob said, taking the box.

"Hey! That thing was huge!" Gavin joked, coming down the ladder and lifting it, closing the attic trap door. "I thought you were meeting us at the Davises."

"I know. And I'll go to this thing. But I wanted a moment with Deb without all those people. You know. My sister..."

"Ohhh. Yeah. Of course. I'll give you a moment," Gavin said, taking back the box and heading back out to his car.

He dug his keys out of his pocket. He put the box in the back seat and climbed behind the wheel. He put the key in the ignition and turned it, flipping on the radio and checking radio stations until he found a song he liked. He knocked Deb's purse, sitting on the center console, to the passenger side floorboard with his elbow. "Crap," he said, leaning over to pick it up.

A shot rang out. His driver's side, and then the passenger side, windows exploded. The bullet buried itself in a tree in Deb's neighbor's yard. He threw himself prone against the seats, yelling for Deb and Bob to get down and stay in the house. He opened the passenger side door, punched the glove box, which always stuck, dug around for his spare weapon and magazine, and dove across the seats and out the passenger side, slamming his left shoulder into the car's door frame on his way out. His phone fell to the ground, breaking open when he fell on top of it. He sat on the ground by his front passenger side wheel, slammed the magazine into the weapon, finding he was unable to use his left arm, and chambered a bullet. He spun on his butt to his knee and moved, in one fluid motion, to the front of the car. He then moved, weapon held in front of him, stealthily from one shadow to the next, moving toward where the shot had originated. It was only once he had cleared the yard and knew the shooter had run off in the opposite direction that he felt the sting in his shoulder. "Crap," he said again, noticing the blood.

"You've been shot!" Deb screamed, running to him, fear and panic in her eyes.

"I told you to stay inside," he scolded her.

"He's gone. Uncle Bob saw him run that way," she cried out, pointing in the direction the evidence indicated.

Her lip trembled, and her eyes filled to overflowing. She repeated, this time in a whisper, "You've been shot." The tears ran down her cheeks.

"Hey, Deb. I'm okay. It's a scratch. Probably from the glass. Not the bullet. Okay? Okay?" he said, holstering his weapon and grabbing her shoulder. He winced, moving his arm.

Her tears came faster. She buried her face in his chest and hugged him tightly to her as the police cars surrounded them.

He identified himself, and the officers stood down.

"You know how I said I'm not ready for forever?" she sobbed.

"Yeah," he replied, kissing her forehead when she looked up at him.

"Well, I'm not ready to lose you, either."

"Deb, I'm a cop."

"I know that. Believe me. I know better than most. That's not what I mean," she pleaded.

"What do you mean?"

"I mean, don't leave me."

"Okay. I won't."

CHAPTER 49

"Mom! It smells amazing in here!" Miranda announced, hugging her mother and kissing her cheek. "You know everybody except Jameka and Theo." She motioned to the girls. Jameka stepped forward graciously and offered her hand. Theo did a curtsy and twirled her hair, popping her bubble gum.

"Hello, Mrs. Davis. I'm Jameka Bradley, Dan's...um... sister. You have a lovely home," Jameka said, smiling.

"Miss Teen Maryland, 2023!" Connie announced.

"Yes, Ma'am."

Miranda smiled. "Jameka, this is my mother, Connie Southerland Davis, Miss Teen Illinois, 1985."

Camille cleared her throat.

"Oh, and this is Camille Camacho, Dr. Wise's granddaughter, and that's Liam and Annalise, Camille's children." Miranda plopped down in a chair next to her friend. "Well...two of them," she cooed at Camille's tummy.

"Sam and Pete are in the family room, looking at those DVDs I got in the mail," Connie said to Dan as he leaned in, kissing her on the cheek. He nodded, and he and Tom disappeared through the butler's pantry.

Frank stood with his hands behind his back behind Theo, observing quietly.

Connie grabbed a bottle of Rose' and popped it open.

She poured a giant glass.

"I'd offer to give you all a tour, but I'm pooped," Miranda said, laying her head on the table. "It's been a day. I need a minute. And a glass of wine." Her mother sat the glass in front of her even as she spoke the words.

"Theo, Frank? Wine? Or something harder? There's a full bar in the family room," Connie offered.

Frank pointed toward the butler's pantry.

"Yes, straight through to the dining room. Turn left. Can't miss it." Connie answered his unspoken question.

"I'll have some of the Rose'. Thank ya," Theo replied, sitting next to Miranda.

Connie poured out another glass.

The gate buzzed. Connie looked at her phone. The chauffeur announced his passengers. She buzzed him in.

As Ava and Angelica joined the growing group in the kitchen, over the noise of the greetings and introductions, Dan's voice rang out, "FUCK! IS HE OKAY? WHERE'S KATELYNN AND JASON?"

As if in answer to that question, Katelynn's car drove up to the gate.

"What was that about?" Katelynn asked as she came in through the kitchen door. "Dan ran out of the house before I even pulled into the driveway. He pulled Jason out of the car, hugged him, and ran back inside carrying him."

"I don't know," Miranda said, standing and running through the living room. She found Dan sitting on the third step in the entrance hall, hugging Jason and breathing deeply.

"What?" she asked, frightened by the look on his face. Something was wrong.

"Somebody took a shot at Gavin in Deb's driveway," he replied.

"Gavin was shot?" she yelled.

Her question drew all the people in the house to the entrance hall. They all stood there looking at Dan.

"He has a shoulder wound. He says he thinks it is a cut. He got some glass in his arm from the car window shattering. He leaned down to pick up Deb's purse, which he'd knocked on the floor of the car at just the right time." He was quiet for a minute; then he continued, "Sue says it looks like a bullet wound to her. The glass shattered, but car windows are tempered; they don't tend to cut you like that."

"And Deb's okay?" asked Katelynn, panicking.

"Deb's okay. Bob, too. They were in the house," he answered, kissing Jason's head.

He looked up and noticed his stepmother and Angelica. "Ava! Ms. Frost! Hi! Sorry. I…"

Angelica held up her hand, "It's okay. Sounds like somebody you care about was hurt. Introductions can wait a minute." That was kind. Miranda thought she was going to like Angelica Frost.

He nodded. "I'm so sorry. I brought you here because I wanted you out of the way of Kris Bowen. And you don't even have any clothes. I won't keep you here against your will, but I really recommend you stay here until we get this guy."

"Yes, I think I agree. But where will you put us all?" Angelica laughed.

"There are four empty bedrooms upstairs and two more in the apartment. Miranda and Dan have an extra room, too. I'm sure we can accommodate you and Jameka, Ms. Frost," Sam said.

CHAPTER 50

Dan led Angelica and Jameka to the apartment. "Stairs or elevator?" he asked.

"Stairs are okay," Angelica answered, shaking her head. She grabbed Jameka's arm. "Oh, my GAWD!" she mouthed.

Dan headed up the steps, entered the code on the alarm system, and unlocked the door. He flipped on the lights, grabbed the window shade remote, and lowered the shades.

Connie had redecorated after he'd moved out. The furniture was all sleek and modern but somehow still feminine. Jason's baby bedroom was redone into a grown-up guest room with a queen-sized sleigh bed in purple tones. His bedroom looked much the same. Of course, it had been Mike's room first, and that was how it had looked when he moved in.

He took his credit card out, handing it to Angelica.

"Jameka has her laptop. Order anything you want, whatever clothes you need, anything. You can get underwear, pajamas, and anything you need immediately delivered from Target or Walmart. Anything else might take a day or so," he said.

"What's my budget?" she asked.

"There's no limit. Spend whatever you want."

Angelica shook her head. "Your stepmother asked if I

wanted one of the Escalades you just gave her."

"Oh, sure. If you want."

"She said you'd paid Jameka's tuition for next year already," she continued.

"Yes, ma'am. And I am instructing my lawyer...who you just met...to set up a trust fund for her."

"You are? Why?" interrupted Jameka.

He looked at her and smiled. "Because my dad always took care of my every need. He's not here to take care of yours. I am."

"You don't even know us, Mr. Bradley," Angelica said.

"I'm just Dan. Danny, if the mood suits you. I knew my father. Obviously, I didn't know everything about him, but I knew him. He trusted you. I trust you."

"Just like that?" Angelica asked.

"Just like that," he answered.

He sat down on the sofa. "Please, sit down, Ms. Frost. I'll answer any questions I can."

She sat in the recliner and crossed her feet at the ankles. "Okay. Your daddy. Jameka's daddy sent me $1400 a month in child support. Was I entitled to more?"

"No. That sounds right. He wasn't wealthy. He was a truck driver."

"You lived in this neighborhood?"

"Yes. Across the street. This is a middle-class neighborhood. This house...is the exception. Mr. Davis is an attorney. A partner. Miranda grew up here. I grew up across the street," he smiled.

"Where'd you get your money?"

"It's a long story. Most of it was covered in the Tribune. You can look it up. But the short version is my mother's biological mother left it to me. She left me everything. And everything was a lot."

"You don't feel guilty takin' it from her family?"

"Since they murdered my mother and baby sister when I was five and tried to kill Miranda and would have killed me, no. Not really."

"What kind of work did you do before you got rich?"

"I am still a deputy sheriff with the Kane County Sheriff's Department. I head the investigations department."

Angelica stared at him. "Well, your answers match what Ms. Ava told me."

"Do you really think Kris Bowen would hurt us?" Jameka interjected.

"To hurt me, yes."

"Why does he want to hurt you?" Angelica asked.

"Jealousy. Greed. He's my cousin."

"Your cousin?" Jameka exclaimed.

"My biological grandparents are his biological grandparents. So biologically, yes," he answered.

"But he's rich on his own. Why does he need what you got?" Angelica pointed out.

Dan shrugged. "He feels like he deserves it more than I do, I guess. So? The apartment? Does this work for you?"

"Dan, it's bigger than my house," Angelica laughed.

CHAPTER 51

"I told you; you were shot," Deb said, looking hard at Gavin. She hoped it was hard anyway. He had a way of making her melt into a puddle.

The doctor finished the stitches and took out a shoulder immobilizer for his arm.

"Oh, come on! Why do I need this thing?" Gavin complained.

"Because you dislocated your shoulder diving into the driveway, and you have soft tissue damage from the bullet grazing you, Officer Mahoney, and if you don't wear it, I'll sic your girlfriend there on you," replied the doctor smugly.

"He'll wear it!" Deb growled.

"I'll wear it," he acquiesced.

The doctor bandaged the wound. The nurse helped him get his tee shirt on. To Deb's mind, the nurse took a little too long helping him into that tee shirt. The doctor fitted the immobilizer and sling around his waist and attached his arm at the wrist, leaving the shoulder free so that nothing rubbed the wound.

"You can take it off to shower and dress. Otherwise, leave it on. Even when you're sleeping. Four weeks, minimum. Maybe six weeks," the doctor instructed.

"Great. At least it's my left arm."

The doctor chuckled. "Take it easy for six weeks, okay?

Light duty."

"Ugg!" Gavin groaned.

The nurse handed Deb the release paperwork. They walked together out to the Emergency Room waiting area. Bob was sitting alone, waiting for them. As they emerged from the double doors, he stood and motioned for them to wait while he got his car.

"Please tell me he doesn't drive a hearse," Gavin said.

Deb clamped her mouth shut.

"Seriously? A hearse?"

"A 1964 Cadillac Hearse. Sorry."

"Banner evening!" he grumbled as the automatic door swooshed open in front of them, and they walked through together.

The hearse pulled up to the curb, and they both climbed into the front bench seat. The file box was tucked in the back, just behind the seat. Deb, sitting in the middle, giggled. Then she kissed Uncle Bob's cheek. Turning to Gavin, she grabbed his face with both hands and kissed him full on the mouth. Bob put the hearse in drive and pulled away.

CHAPTER 52

Deb, Gavin, and Bob arrived at the Davis home to find Connie had held dinner for them, feeding only the children. Everyone was starving, Connie explained.

"So…what'd we miss?" joked Gavin as he sat down beside Deb at the dining room table.

Gavin stared at his knife and at the chicken on the serving platter. Deb wordlessly placed two drumsticks on his plate and winked at him. She grabbed a biscuit, sliced it open, and buttered it, placing it beside the chicken on his plate.

"Green beans?" she asked. She spooned some on her plate and turned to look at him.

"Sure, Mom," he answered, embarrassed. She spooned a serving on his plate and passed the bowl behind him to Theo on his left.

She repeated the process with mashed potatoes, gravy, and fruit salad. It was awkward for Gavin, but he was starving, and the food was good, so he endured it. Besides, that bullet had passed inches from his head. He was so relieved to just be there, though he was trying to keep that to himself. Still, he kept reliving the moment the windows shattered over and over in his mind, becoming more and more circumspective as the night wore on.

He hadn't called his parents. He'd always called his parents after any close call to let them know he was okay, but this close call was just a little too close. He couldn't talk about it just now, not with the sound of Private First-Class Evan Hondo, 19, fresh out of high school, coughing up blood among the yells of the soldiers and the ricochet of bullets thundering in his brain.

And then there was Deb. She'd been there. After what happened to Mark, for her to have been there felt horribly unfair to him. He needed time to collect himself, to hold his girl, to feel okay for a minute.

The shoulder immobilizer was massively uncomfortable, and his back and shoulder felt stiff. He shifted in his seat. Windows shattered. His face in the driveway. His shoulder stinging. Deb's face. "Don't Leave me." Deb's face. Evan's face. Deb's face. Deb's tears. His tears.

"Dan, can we do this tomorrow?" Deb suddenly asked.

Gavin looked up to find all eyes on him. He realized that he'd grabbed his knife and had stabbed the chicken on his plate. Hard enough to have broken the plate.

"Oh. I'm...sorry. I don't know what I...I'll pay for it," he stammered, trying with his one hand to gather the pieces of broken plate and food up. Deb grabbed his hand.

"I'll get it," she said, letting go of his hand.

"It's okay, Gavin. The plate's just a plate. Are you okay?" Connie asked, clearly concerned.

He laughed a little maniacally. "Apparently not." He took a deep breath. "Yeah, I'm okay. I'm just...angry. I'm sorry I took it out on your dinnerware."

"Yeah. It's late. And you need to get your head together. You want to stay here?" Dan asked.

Gavin shook his head.

Dan took his key fob out of his pocket and tossed it to Deb. "Take my Escalade. I'm staying here tonight, anyway."

"Yes, we're quite exhausted," Frank started.

"We'll go to my place tonight," Bob continued.

"If you wouldn't mind," Frank began.

"Letting Theo stay here," Bob finished.

Tom was sitting next to Angelica. He leaned toward her. "That's creepy, right?" he whispered.

"What? The Vincent Price twins talking like one person? Yeah. That's creepy," she whispered back.

"I'd have gone with Belo Lugosi over Vincent Price, but I get you," he smiled. "I can't believe Kathy was the normal one."

"Who's Kathy?" Angelica asked.

"Well, I'm in good company anyway," Gavin said. "Everybody here is a little crazy."

CHAPTER 53

Dave Mahoney saw the fugitive alert. "Officer-involved shooting, Batavia, Illinois. Suspect described as Caucasian male. Average Height. Overweight. 50 – 60 years old. Beard. Off-duty State Trooper ambushed and wounded." He waited for the call. Gavin would call to tell him he was fine, that it was a different state trooper. Only he didn't.

Dave started to pace the Police Department. From the front entrance, through the office, through the 911 dispatch to the holding cells, and back again. Over and over again.

His sister-in-law, Tami, was working dispatch overnight. "Dave, you're wearing a trench in the floor," she said after his fourth or fifth pass. "Just call him."

"I tried. It goes straight to voicemail," he answered, exasperated.

"Then call the Elgin office," she suggested.

"Oh, God, no. If it's not him, then he'll never live that down." He wrung his hands.

"He's good friends with Brandon's sister, Deb. Call her." That was true. He was always talking about Deb. He and Deb took her kid to Brookfield Zoo. Or he and Deb saw that movie last week. Or he and Deb went to the range. Gavin talked more about Deb than anything else lately.

"It's awfully late," he said, hesitating, but he was considering it.

"Well, it's either that or you hit bedrock," she quipped, pointing at the floor.

"Do you have her number?"

"Just use my phone," she said, handing it to him.

He called the number. It rang four times.

"Mmmmm. Hello," came the sleep-laden answer.

"Ms. Bradley. I'm so sorry to wake ya. This is Dave Mahoney. I've been tryin' to reach Gavin, and…I'm worried." His brogue, usually almost undetectable, sounded heavy, heavy enough for him to hear it himself.

"Oh. Hi, Mr. Mahoney. His phone busted. Sorry. I should have made him call you. It just slipped my mind. Gavin. Gavin. Wake up. It's your dad."

Dave's eyes widened. Well, that certainly explained all the talk about Deb. Tami mouthed, "What?"

"Dad?" came Gavin's voice.

"Gavin?" Dave asked. Tami's mouth dropped open, and she slapped her knee several times. "Gavin, I was worried. I saw this fugitive alert…"

"I'm okay, Dad. Just a flesh wound. The dislocated shoulder hurts more than the bullet. And this damned immobilizer thing is uncomfortable. But I'm okay."

"Shoulder… bullet…WOUNDED? WHY THE HELL DIDN'T YA CALL?"

"You're right, Dad. I should have called. I'm sorry."

CHAPTER 54

Dan had trouble sleeping. After an hour, he got up and retrieved the file box. He hauled it up to the reading nook and sat on the sofa, sighing at the sight of the blood splatter across the lid. Thank God the wound was superficial. Mike's senior picture grinned that goofy, toothy, not-a-smile-smile at him from the wall. Not everyone had been so lucky.

"What's with the DVDs, Mike?" he asked the picture.

Carmen jumped on top of the box. She did a little cat circle, meowed, and reared up on her rear legs, batting at some invisible cat toy she conjured to capture Dan's attention. He chuckled and patted her head. He picked her up, setting her on the sofa beside him, and opened the box.

Kathy had worked at Geneli back in 1991. But she had had access to Salvatore for the last 20 years, and access to Salvatore was access to Geneli. As Deb had suspected, her mother had indeed grabbed files she felt could be beneficial to her and her daughters over the years. The Campana parking lot file, where Salvatore claimed he'd gotten rid of Roger Kaminski's body, was in the box.

Dan ran his finger along the file tabs. A chill ran down his spine, and he shivered. The tab was unlabeled on the file where his hand had stopped. He pulled it out and opened it, curious, as it appeared to be the only file without a label. Mike's senior picture grinned at him from inside the file folder. *What the hell?*

He flipped the page. Miranda's senior picture. He flipped the page again. Sally Blevins. The file was a detailed report on the Batavia High School "You're Never Alone" teen suicide prevention initiative, 2010-2011 school year, prepared by a private detective out of Chicago for Geneli Architecture, presumably in contemplation of a donation to the program. However, the PI had investigated the founding board thoroughly in this report, more than any simple philanthropic interest would demand.

"WHOA!" he yelled, jumping up, wanting to punch... something...anything. "GOD DAMN MOTHER..."

Every door opened.

"AAAAAAAAAAAAAAAAGGGGGGGGGGG!" he screamed, breaking down into tears.

"Jesus! Dan! What's wrong?" asked Tom, being the first to reach his side.

Dan, unable to speak as he was openly sobbing, handed the FBI agent the file and pointed.

"Let's see. What am I looking at? Um...A PI report on..." The agent looked over at Miranda standing in the door to the guest room. "There's a note: M. Davis attending UMW in the fall. S. Geneli should forward report to K. Bowen to handle retribution."

"Wh-what?" Miranda stammered, sinking to the floor. "Retribution for what?"

Dan had regained his composure enough to speak. "I'll fucking kill him," he hissed.

"Not if I get to him first," Sam said, rushing to his daughter.

CHAPTER 55

Gavin handed Deb back her phone. "My family is going to descend on us like a black horde."

"Hmmm. Nice cosplay reference."

"Yeah, I thought so," he smiled. He slipped his free arm under her waist and pulled her close. She was lying on her side facing him. She bit her bottom lip, leaning in to kiss his neck.

"I don't mind. Let the black horde descend. As long as you're on my team," she whispered against his skin. "Can I ask you something?"

"Anything, DeBella," he replied, closing his eyes.

"When was the last time you had sex?"

He opened his eyes. "Have you hit your head?" he laughed.

She elbowed his ribs. "I mean before me!"

"November 25," he answered.

"Who was she?"

"Nobody of any consequence."

"You must have liked her," she said.

"We went out two or three times. It was nothing."

"What's her name?"

"Lisa Granger. She's a bartender."

"Why haven't you…since November," she asked.

"I didn't want to," he said.

"But you said you would have any time I wanted," she persisted.

"Jesus, Deb. What do you want me to say?"

"That you didn't want to because you wanted me."

"Well, that's pretty fucking obvious, isn't it?" he laughed. Was she jealous? Deb had eye-balled that nurse awfully hard when her hand had lingered on his torso a little longer than necessary. And that poor waitress the other day.

"Yeah, but a girl likes to hear it," she said smugly.

"Fine. I only wanted to be with you, so I didn't call Lisa or anybody else."

"Cool!" she laughed. She snuggled down into the crook of his uninjured arm. He closed his eyes again. They lay quietly for a moment. She took a deep breath and said, "Gavin, do you have PTSD?" Crap, he thought. He wasn't ready for this conversation.

"No. Not really. I have survivor's guilt more than anything. I came through unscathed. Not everybody I know and love did. My cousin, Horatio, was pretty badly wounded. And there was a kid from Dixon. Evan Hondo. He didn't come home. I don't like thinking about it. I don't like talking about it. But I don't have anxiety from it."

"You kind of glazed over before you broke that plate."

"That wasn't about Afghanistan. That was about you. I don't like seeing you hurt," he lied sleepily.

"I wasn't the one hurt," she whispered.

"Hmmmm," he said, falling back to sleep, breathing in her scent.

******

She closed her eyes, holding him tightly. She found she didn't want to let go of him. She was doing it again. Falling. Too hard. Too fast. But it felt different this time. In her mind, she saw it clearly. Dan had been at the top of the cliff and held her by her hand as she hung over the side. He tried to keep her up. Mark ran hand in hand with her and jumped off the cliff. Gavin was waiting at the bottom, ready to catch her. The falling wasn't scary, knowing he was there. She drifted off to sleep pondering the thought: How had he gotten to the bottom of the cliff?

At 6:30 am, Deb was awakened by the incessant knocking at Gavin's apartment door. He groaned in his sleep as she extricated herself from his embrace, his face showing the pain. She smiled and ran to the door. She looked through the peephole. A man, a woman, mid-fifties to sixty, Brandon towering behind them. *Ah, the black horde.*

She undid the chain lock and opened the door. "Shhhhh, read him the riot act later. Let him sleep right now. Come in."

They filed in, Brandon stooping through the door frame. "Hey, Marlon Brando," she said, patting him on his shoulder as he averted his eyes. "What's wrong?"

"Geez, Debbie. Like I want my sister answering the door in my cousin's tee shirt and nuthin' else," he whined.

"Deb! So nice to meet you," the woman exclaimed gleefully, excitedly. "I'm Gabriella Mahoney, Gavin's mama." She grabbed Deb by her shoulders and kissed both cheeks. "Oh, this is my husband, Dave."

Brandon stared at the Wall.

"Yo, Brandon? Would you be more comfortable if I put on some clothes?" Deb laughed. He nodded furiously.

"Be right back," she smiled at Gavin's mother, who laughed nervously in response.

"You made her uncomfortable!" Gabriella admonished her nephew.

He turned and looked at his aunt, flabbergasted, "Tia Gabbie. Nothing makes her uncomfortable. If she were uncomfortable, she'd have gotten dressed before she answered the door!"

Deb cracked up from the hallway, overhearing their comments. She walked into Gavin's room and quietly rummaged through the pile of clothes on the floor. The pile was out of place in the tidy room, but she had undressed them both since he couldn't use his arm, and the floor was where she had thrown the discarded clothing. She found her jeans, bra, and shirt and put them on.

"That's going to drive me crazy," he grumbled from the bed.

"Oh yeah? Don't get shot!" She sat on the edge of the bed. He sat up, wincing and grabbing his shoulder. He kissed her.

"Yeah. I'll remember that in the future." He groaned. "What's up?"

"The black horde."

"Ug. Okay. Get me a shirt and jeans, please. From the closet, not the floor, thank you."

"No. Go back to sleep. I'll handle it."

He smiled. "No, Deb. This is my mess. I knew my dad would see that BOLO. I should have called. Shirt. Jeans. Please."

She sighed and stood, walking to his closet. "What kind of maniac irons his tee shirts?" she joked, pulling out a button-down shirt and pair of Levis.

He teased back. "I'm surprised you bothered to get dressed. You aren't the bashful type."

"Heh. I didn't. But Brandon wouldn't look at me."

"Brandon? Great. I wonder if I'm dealing with my cousin or your brother."

She took off his shoulder immobilizer and helped him slip into the shirt.

"He's both, Honey," she smiled and kissed him as she buttoned his shirt, letting her own hands linger on his abdomen muscles. He gave her a knowing look that said she was wrong.

"Maybe so. But my cousin would congratulate me for the hot blonde in my bed. Your brother, on the other hand, is going to pummel me."

"You are both aware that I am a grown woman?"

"Well, I am," he chuckled.

"Seriously, I have a kid and everything. Pretty much dispels any misconceptions about my being a virgin."

"Uh-huh. He's still going to pummel me. Ow, damnit!" he complained as she put the immobilizer back on him a little roughly. He pulled on his jeans, tucked in the shirt, and headed out. She followed him.

CHAPTER 56

Dan drank his fifth cup of coffee. Connie started a new pot. Dan had been through the box several more times. Kathy did not have any Geneli memo regarding his mother or sister. Nothing on Moore Industries or Moore Robotics either. Just the ominous file on the anti-suicide campaign Mike and Miranda had founded with the note suggesting Miranda's rape had been some sort of contracted retribution.

Jameka and Angelica emerged from the apartment and crossed the drive and patio, knocking on the back door.

"Good morning," Angelica sang, coming through the door.

Dan grumbled several expletives under his breath.

"I beg your pardon?" Angelica said, looking harshly in his direction.

"Ignore him, Angelica," Connie said, offering a cup of coffee to their guest. "He's not cussing at you. He's cussing at... Is he cussing at Salvatore or Kris?"

"Both." Miranda yawned. "I don't understand what an anti-suicide campaign founded in the memory of Wayne Carver has to do with any of this."

"Huh, that's a coincidence," Jameka offered, taking a cup from Connie.

Dan looked up, snapping to attention. "There's no such thing. It's probably important. The last six months has proven that to me."

"Um…okay. Well, I used a quote from a lawsuit filed against Bowen by a Wayne Carver in my paper. He was a young African American boy, 14, I think. His parents had dumped him on his grandma, who was raising him. She died from lung cancer. He had a really strong case against Bowen Tobacco. But he committed suicide, so nothing came of it."

Dan and Miranda stared at Jameka with their mouths open.

"Um. Connie. Do you have any boxes that might contain 'You're Not Alone' stuff?" asked Dan.

"Dan, I have everything," Connie replied.

Theo came through the butler's pantry. "Oh, hello, everybody. What a night," she said.

"Sorry, Theo. I couldn't sleep," Dan said. "Miranda, can you call Mary Cummings? See if she did send that package to your mom."

"Sure," Miranda yawned again.

"I have a cousin named Mary Cummings. Isn't that funny?"

Jameka leaned forward. "Is that another one of those things that doesn't exist?"

"I'm willing to guarantee it," Dan replied with a smile. "Theodosia Zamphir Bowen? You have a cousin named Mary Cummings?"

"Sure. My mama's sister's kid. My mama grew up in that Podunk town y'all were staying in. My mama left her a house there, in fact, when she died. Some lawyer at the office Mary worked at helped Mama draw up the will."

Dan facepalmed. "Was his name Mike Davis?" he asked through his fingers.

"Yeah, something like that. Michael, Micky, Mitch. I don't know."

He lowered his hand. "Have you ever seen him?"

"Sure. I brought my mama to Chicago to meet him. March, 2022. Weird guy. Wouldn't look us in the eyes. Rocked back and forth. Talked like a robot. But he was nice. Just quirky."

Dan stared at her, dumbfounded. "Think, Theo. Do you see a picture of him in this room?"

She glanced around the room and pointed to the collage of snapshots Connie had posted on her refrigerator door with magnets. "Hey, yeah, that's him." She looked around the room at the flabbergasted faces staring back at her. "What?"

Dan turned back to Miranda. "Never mind."

CHAPTER 57

Gavin explained everything to his dad over breakfast at Batavia Diner. Apologies went better with pancakes.

"It would be nice if you cooked next time we visit, Deb," Gabriella said. "I'd love to see your home."

Deb choked on her coffee. "Uh. Sure, but I kind of suck in the kitchen. You're welcome at my house anytime, but trust me, you'll prefer to eat out."

"Nonsense! I'll teach you," Gabriella declared.

Gavin covered his mouth with his hand and turned to look out the window. Deb kicked him under the table.

Brandon snickered, "She'll teach you, Debbie."

"Uhhhhhh. Sure. Sounds like fun."

He was grateful when Deb's phone rang. His mother was making this so awkward. Deb looked at it and stood. "Sorry. It's the funeral home. I have to take this." She walked outside quickly, taking the call.

"Funeral home?" Gavin's mother asked, leaning toward him.

"Yeah, Mom. Her mother was murdered two days ago. Kind of what we've been talking about for the last forty-five minutes," he replied, trying not to laugh.

"Oh. I never listen to the gory details, Sweetheart. I just wait for the part where you're okay."

"Good to know, Mom," he chuckled, unable to contain

himself any longer.

"I like her. Don't screw this one up," she whispered.

"I like her, too. I'll try not to," he whispered back.

"I'm fine with it," Brandon announced.

They all turned and looked at him.

"No. Really. I am. Just ask her to put her clothes on before she answers the door."

"Dude! I'm not touching that with a ten-foot pole. She's your sister. You tell her!" Gavin replied, sipping his orange juice through a straw.

"I swear to God, Gav! Don't push it! She's my sister! I'm trying to be understanding here, but you really gotta go after my sister?" Brandon's temper was starting to rise again.

"Please. She's a grown woman. And you didn't even know she existed until I found her."

"What's your point?" Brandon growled.

"That...I saw her first!" Gavin shot back.

Brandon and Gavin stared at each other over the table. Anger registered on both their faces.

Then, they both cracked up. "You saw her first? Really? So, you started working on her before you knew she was my sister?"

"Well...kinda," Gavin blushed. "And you kinda helped, so back off."

"I helped? How?"

Gavin's eyes flashed. "You asked that girl to dare her to kiss me. You and Freddy. Jokers. Bet you didn't think I knew that."

"What the fu...heck...are you talkin' about? Asked what girl?"

"The slutty nurse," Gavin replied, leaning back in his chair.

"I'm talkin' about DeBella, and you're talkin' about

what…Some girl 10 or so years ago at a Halloween party? I did you a favor. That girl was hot, and you couldn't take your eyes off her."

"It was 11 years ago. And yes, you did. So, get over it now and shut up." Gavin huffed.

"I have no idea what you're talking about!" Brandon exclaimed in exasperation.

Dave put his head in his hand and shook it. "Brandon. It appears your sister would be the very girl at the party."

Brandon looked at Gavin for a moment. "Deb was Morticia?"

Gavin nodded, looking out the window at her by the Escalade they had borrowed from Dan.

"I dared my sister to make out with you?"

Gavin nodded.

"I laughed like a fool when she did it."

Gavin nodded.

"Okay. Let's not talk about that. So, this friend of yours…he's really the kid that…you know…his mom and baby sister…?" Brandon changed the subject. He was blushing. The big oaf.

Gavin nodded. "Yeah, that's him."

"Melissa's dad was just talking about that the other day, you know, with Jason staying with us and all…not in front of Jason, though!" Brandon continued. "Brian worked with Keith Bradley at the mill, you know."

"Oh, yeah? Did he know him well?" Gavin asked.

"Says he did. He told me they went out to dinner with Keith and Ellen at Candlelight like the night before. He said Keith was scared, and Ellen told him it was going to be fine. He said Keith was telling her not to trust Wally, brother or not, that he got a bad feeling from him. She told him he was being paranoid."

Gavin sat up. "Brian said Keith talked about Wally? The night BEFORE Ellen was killed?"

"Yeah, why? Is that important? I thought Geno Geneli killed her." Brandon said.

"He did, but there may have been more people involved," Gavin said, standing. "Sorry, I gotta go. Do me a favor, Brandon: get Brian to call me. Today." He pulled out his wallet, flipped it open, and stared at it.

"I got the check, Son," Dave said with a laugh.

"Thanks, Dad. I'll get it next time. I hate this stupid thing."

"Well, don't get shot," his mother quipped.

"It's not for the gunshot. That's literally just a scratch. It's because I dislocated my shoulder diving out of the car," he explained.

"Well, don't do that!"

"I was taking cover from gunfire," he continued.

"Oh. Well, DO THAT!"

CHAPTER 58

Connie led Dan to the attic. She flipped on the light to reveal the most well-organized attic in the world. "Mike's stuff is over there. Over his room," she said, pointing.

"I got that," Dan said, noting the hand-carved wooden sign hanging from the rafters over that portion of the attic that read, "Mike."

He looked around. There were similar signs hanging over the appropriate spaces that read, "Miranda," "Sam," "Connie," "Wedding gifts," "Bathroom," "Living room," "Family Room," "Kitchen," and "Dining Room." There were rows and rows of shelves under the signs, and there were boxes neatly stacked on all the shelves.

"I believe you may be slightly OCD, Connie," he teased.

"You'll thank me later," she quipped back.

He made his way to the shelves marked "Mike."

"Yep, the boxes are labeled by subject and date," he nodded. "Thanks, Connie," he called over his shoulder as she headed back down the stairs.

"Told you so!" she called back.

He found the boxes labeled "You're Never Alone." Then, he noticed a subset of boxes labeled "Wayne Carver." He started with those. What he discovered in them blew him away. Mike had saved everything. Everything. This is going to take forever, he thought.

He called out, "Hey, Jameka!"

Jameka appeared at the foot of the attic stairs. "Yeah?"

"Who was Wayne Carver's attorney in that lawsuit?" he yelled.

"Terrence Park," she yelled back. "Why?"

"Because he's one of Sam's partners," Dan replied. Then he added under his breath, "And he's how Mike got the Bowens to back off Miranda. Mike used him as a threat."

He pulled down the "Wayne Carver" boxes and the "You're Never Alone" boxes. That's when he saw a dust-covered box hidden behind the others. The handwriting on it was Mike's, not Connie's. He'd labeled it "Ellen/Elaine Bradley."

"What the...?" Dan mumbled as he pulled it out, too.

He started carrying the boxes down to the family room, where Tom was setting up his command center again. He passed Miranda on the stairs down to the entrance hall. She moved past him without so much as a smile and went into the guest room, closing the door.

He deposited the box he was carrying on the floor by the French doors leading to the family room and bounded back up the stairs. He knocked at the door and opened it.

"Yeah?" she said, turning to him. She was sitting on the bed.

"Is something wrong?" he asked, concerned.

"No. Just a headache," she said.

He entered the room, closing the door behind him, and sat beside her.

"I've been distracted the last few days, my Love. I'm sorry," he said, rubbing her head.

"Well, of course, you've been preoccupied. Your ex-mother-in-law died in your arms, your best friend has been wounded, oh, and you have a sister your dad never told you about. I understand."

He kissed her cheek. "And yet, you're more important to me than any of that," he whispered.

She finally smiled and laid her head on his shoulder. "I'm supposed to be excited about my wedding. I'm supposed to be worried about centerpieces and who sits at which table, whether to order the beef or chicken, whether the flowers match the dresses just enough. Instead, I've got a crazy man threatening me...again...and you have barely noticed me, which I realize sounds stupid and entitled, but there it is."

He laughed. "I'm so sorry. You deserve everything you're missing. And I'm trying my damnedest to get it back for you."

She nuzzled his neck, and he turned to her, kissing her for the first time in what felt like days, really kissing her. God, he'd missed her.

She wrapped her arms around his neck. He moved his hands down to her waist, pulling her against him. Her breath caught in her chest as he kissed her deeper.

"Daddy?" said Jason, suddenly standing at his knee.

He pulled away, reluctantly. "Hey, Sweetheart. What's up?"

"Can you play with me? I'm bored!" he whined.

"Bored? Are you kidding me?" Dan said, grabbing the boy in his arms, tossing him onto the bed, and tickling him.

Jason laughed and squirmed.

Dan pretended to gnaw on the boy's neck. Then he kissed his forehead and lay down beside him. "Mommy should be here soon, Angel. Daddy, Gavin, and Uncle Tom have some work to do."

"Is Uncle Tom reawee my uncle?" the boy asked, obviously confused by his rapidly expanding family.

"Yes. He's Uncle Frank and Uncle Bob's brother.

Grandma was his sister," Dan answered.

"And Aunt Jameka?" he asked.

"Well, Aunt Katie is Mommy's sister, right?"

"Yas," he nodded.

"And Uncle Brandon is Mommy's brother, right?"

"Yas."

"Well, Aunt Jameka is Daddy's sister."

"Who is Angewica to me, then?" he asked, clearly confused.

Dan furrowed his brow. "Well, who is Tami?"

"Tami is Uncle Brandon's mommy. She's nice, but she's not related to me."

"Same thing."

"Ohhhhhh. I see." Then he grinned. "And if Mommy mawwees Gabin, he'll be my stepdaddy, like Nana is going to be my stepmommy, and Granny Ava is your stepmommy."

"Um. Yeah," Dan answered, uncertain how to address Gavin and Deb's relationship with his son, "But Gavin and Mommy are just starting to...date...they're not ready to get married yet."

"Oh, I knows. But Nana's brother told me they will."

Dan looked at Miranda, who shrugged and shook her head.

"Honey, Nana's brother died when you were very little. I don't think you can remember him, and it was before any of us knew Gavin."

The boy rolled his eyes. "I knows that, Daddy."

From below, they heard Deb and Gavin coming in and greeting Tom.

"Mommy!!!!!" Jason yelled, jumping off the bed and running to greet his mother.

"Well, that was weird," Dan observed.

Miranda smiled. "Or the truth."

He looked at her with a side-eye. "You believe in ghosts, Miranda?"

"I believe we are more than our bodies," she replied, lying beside him and kissing him.

"I thought you had a headache," he said.

"I did," she replied.

CHAPTER 59

Tuesday morning, Benji, as his father called him, looked across his desk at Pete Camacho. He'd liked the young man's resume five years ago. He'd offered him a job at the time, but it was a step down from the position Pete held at the company he was employed by at that time. Unfortunately, he hadn't the experience required for the director position, and nothing else was available at Moore.

Sadly, each Director of Engineering Moore had hired over the last five years had moved on rather quickly. Meanwhile, Pete kept trying and getting more experience. Benji liked his resolve and had decided to hire him. When Pete mentioned his connection to Dan Bradley, it had no effect on Benji's decision, but it certainly piqued his interest. He'd like to meet the man, given their relationship.

Benji's earliest memory of Dominica Geneli had been at a party back at the University of Illinois when his dad had been an Associate Professor of American Literature. Lilith, Benji's mother, adored parties. She hosted them weekly. And Dominica was a guest at one of those affairs. She was a sophomore at the time.

Benji hadn't understood that it was inappropriate for Dominica to be at the party or the animosity between the pretty girl and his mother, he just found the girl to be pretty, and he liked the toy truck she'd gifted him.

Ben may have only been an Associate Professor, but he was Benjamin Moore's son. And the Moores were old Chicago money. The University had worked hard to attract Ben, and they worked hard to keep him happy. Dominica kept Ben happy. Lilith, on the other hand, was outraged to learn Ben had followed Dominica to Champaign.

Now, at 68, Benji understood his mother's dislike and anger. But he had long ago decided they'd all have been better off if she'd simply left Ben.

"How's it going, Pete? The job, that is," he asked after a long awkward silence. "I can't believe that Bowen kid got in here and did that to you."

"Can't you?" Pete asked.

How much does he know? Benji wondered.

"I used to be good friends with Walter Bowen, but I learned what kind of man he was, and we cut all ties, business or otherwise, with the Bowens a quarter of a century ago. I didn't even know what Kris Bowen looked like. I'm truly sorry he marred your first experience here."

Pete looked confused. "Well, I'm doing okay, I guess. It took a little time for people to trust me, but I'm good at my job."

"You are. And we hope you'll be happy here," Benji smiled. "I'm moving my son, Cameron, into your department. He's my youngest. Just graduated from Stamford last year. He's talented. I believe you can turn him into a top-notch engineer."

"Um, okay," Pete replied. "Am I training my replacement?"

"What? No. Cameron's fresh out of his master's program. You're training an employee, just like any other employee," Benji smiled.

******

Pete shook Benji's hand and left the office.

He looked back over his shoulder and said with a laugh to Mrs. Winters, Benji's executive assistant, "Is he a good guy or a bad guy?"

"What day is it?" she asked with a smirk.

Back in his office, Pete stared at the discs. He wished he could have been more helpful. All he could tell Sam and Connie was that the videos from their own security camera fifteen years ago had been recorded on a closed-circuit device. Their camera at that time had not been connected to the internet. The video capture was recorded on a disc, just like the ones "Mike" had sent to Connie...but these were not the original; they'd been burned to these discs from the original or another burned copy. It was impossible to tell.

As for the video of Ivan, he was flummoxed. He confirmed that Connie was correct that the man in the video was absolutely not Benjamen Moore, III, but Ivan Polaski, a clerk and long-time employee at Moore Robotics. He could offer no insights as to what Ivan was doing or why "Mike" had sent it to Connie.

He buried the discs out of sight in his desk drawer, locking it.

He called Margaret into his office.

"Hey, close the door, Margaret. I'm trying to work out some office dynamics, and I don't want people overhearing and maybe getting the wrong idea. Not like I haven't had a rough enough start," he laughed, drawing her in.

He'd been told he had a great smile and a great laugh. Once his kids, who were two adorable little cherubs, had made an appearance, Margaret had opened up to his charms. She smiled and closed the door, sitting across from him at his desk.

He crossed his hands and leaned in. "You've been here for thirty years or so. Nobody is going to know better than you what's going on in this office."

She pshawed and blushed, "Oh, I don't know. Ivan Polaski and Vivian Winters have been here for forty years since the company was founded."

"Are they the employees who've been here the longest? No actual technical people have been here longer?" he winked.

"No. I think Ivan always wanted to move into the technical side of things, but..." and she moved in and whispered, "Mr. Moore doesn't much like Ivan."

"Really? Ivan seems like a very affable man."

"Oh, I've always found him to be a likable guy, but I think it's more family dynamics than anything," she dished. "He's Mr. Moore's cousin. Their mothers are sisters. Mr. Moore hired Ivan at his mother's request, and Ivan does his job, so Mr. Moore's stuck with him," she giggled.

"Wow. Well, Ivan is certainly good at his job, as far as I can see, and beloved by his peers. He's retiring soon, right? That's what I wanted to talk about."

"Ah, that's so nice of you! I was hoping management would step up. Were you thinking of a party? I could arrange a party! I mean it's kind of late notice, what with his retiring next week and all, but I bet I could do it! Ohhhhhh. I've always wanted to do something like this! But Vivian Winters always does it. Of course, with Mr. Moore not liking poor Ivan much, she isn't doing it. Can I arrange a party?" Her excitement overflowed.

"Um. Sure. There is money in the discretionary fund for that sort of thing. I think that sounds great. And I'm sure you'll arrange a great party. When exactly is he retiring?" he asked, taking out his phone to add it to his calendar.

"Next Friday is his last day! Oh, yay! Thanks, Mr. Camacho."

He opened his door, ending his meeting with Margaret, to see the elevators open. Gavin and Dan came off the elevator. Dan waved, and the two started making their way across the floor.

"Who's that?" he heard an engineer ask from his cubicle. Was that guy even trying to be discreet?

"I believe that is Dan Bradley," answered a young woman in the clerical pool equally loudly. "I've seen his picture in the papers. He must be here to see Mr. Moore."

Her face showed genuine shock when Dan Bradley and his friend made their way to Pete's office instead. "Wow, that guy must really be somebody," she mused. Again...so loud. Was he standing in one of those acoustical anomalies in some buildings where you could clearly hear every whisper?

He invited his friends inside and closed the door behind them. For the first time since he'd been forced to wear an explosive vest, Pete Camacho closed the blinds.

CHAPTER 60

Miranda's headache returned. After Dan and Gavin left for Chicago, she returned to the guest room, pulled the curtains, and turned out the lights. Connie made her take some Advil, but more than the Advil, she wanted dark and quiet.

She pulled back the bedclothes and climbed into the bed. It didn't take long for her to fall asleep.

"Miranda! Miranda!" Mike called.

"What do you want, Mike? My head hurts," she said.

"Wake up, Red."

She sighed and sat up in her old bedroom before her mother redecorated. The pink carpet and pink walls were muted by the gray curtains. Her posters covered the walls. It must have been 2007 or 2008, based on her musical taste.

"Am I in high school?" she asked, looking around.

Mike was suddenly sitting beside her like he was when he'd been well, but certainly not in high school.

"I've missed you, Red," he said looking at the wall, rocking slightly back and forth.

"I've missed you, too, Mike," she said, touching his knee.

"I'm sorry. I didn't mean for them to blame you instead of me."

"Blame me for what?" she asked.

"I'm going to destroy them."

"What are you talking about?"

"They destroyed Wayne," he said. "I'm going to destroy them. They took away Dan's mom and sister. I'm going to give Dan everything they have. He...hurt you. I'm going to hurt him."

"Mike, you're not making any sense."

"Of course, I'm not. I'm a dream."

She sat up and was back in the guest room, lying in the bed, under the covers, the lights off, the shades pulled closed.

"Oh, Mike. Don't stick around for whatever this is."

"I'm not. I'm staying to see you happy," she could swear she heard him answer, but it was just in her mind, like when she'd lost her memory, and she'd heard his voice teasing Dan about wearing his emotions on his face.

"2007. 'They destroyed Wayne,'" she said, flipping on the bedside lamp.

She climbed out of the bed and headed to the attic door. She flipped on the lights at the bottom of the stairs and climbed up. Instead of heading to Mike's area, she went to hers.

"2012, 2010, 2007!" She pulled the box down off the shelf and opened it. She dug through it, finding the speech Mike had written but insisted she deliver instead of him at the fall activities assembly at Batavia High School. "Bowen Tobacco destroyed Wayne Carver as surely as they destroyed his grandmother, Mable. When he stood on the precipice, ready to rule the world, they shoved him off. Walter Bowen killed our friend. His fingerprints are all over Wayne Carver's suicide note," she read. Then she sighed heavily. "I thought that was a great metaphor. But stupid me; Mike didn't do metaphors!"

CHAPTER 61

Ivan Polaski saw the two men exit the elevator. Dan Bradley and his State Trooper friend. The friend appeared to have been injured, but otherwise okay. He was wearing some contraption that held his arm to his torso above his belt. Ivan felt the panic start to rise. *What should he do? What do they know? Why are they here?*

Once the door closed behind them and Pete closed the blinds, he hastily exited the office, making his way down to the street. For an older, overweight man, he moved surprisingly quickly. He hailed a cab and jumped in, disappearing into the Chicago midday traffic.

******

Gavin watched him run to the elevators, noting the man obviously didn't realize the blinds were only opaque on one side. From the inside, they could see the entire office. "Who's that?" he asked, rubbing his shoulder with his one good hand.

"That's Ivan Polaski. He's the man in the video mailed to Connie…in Mr. Moore's office," Pete answered. "He's retiring next week."

"I don't think so," Gavin quipped. "Pretty sure that's the asshole who shot at me Sunday night."

"I thought you didn't see him," Pete said, surprised.

"I didn't, but he was captured on Deb's neighbor's

Ring doorbell," he replied. They sent it to Batavia Police this morning. They messaged me and asked me to come look at it. I didn't know who he was. But…yeah, that's the same…"

Benji Moore knocked on Pete's office door.

Pete stood and opened the door with a smile. "Mr. Moore, hello. Meet my friends, Dan Bradley and Gavin Mahoney."

Benji held out his hand to shake Dan's and Gavin's hands.

"Gentlemen. Pleasure," Benji announced. "I was coming to ask Mr. Camacho to lunch. Perhaps I am too late."

"Not at all, Mr. Moore. We have a lot to discuss. Please, join us," Dan said, gritting his teeth, his eyes narrowing.

"We both know I'm not Mr. Moore to you, Dan."

"What should I call you then? Uncle Ben?" There was a touch of disdain in his voice. Gavin didn't blame him. He hadn't had much luck with long-lost uncles.

"Let's just start with Ben," he said, almost sadly.

"Okay, Ben. I apologize."

"By the way, how'd you hurt your arm, Mr. Mahoney?" Benji asked, his voice steady and friendly, with no hint of any malice ringing through.

"Ivan Polaski shot me," Gavin replied. God, he loved doing that. It was fun to watch suspects squirm under his direct approach.

Benji sat down hard. "What? Ivan did what? Why?"

"We were just wondering the same thing," Dan added. "Think we could take a look in his workstation?"

"Sure. It'll all be yours soon enough, anyway."

"I'm perplexed by you, Ben."

"It's okay. I've invested. I've made a good living. I've negotiated a good retirement settlement. I'm not losing anything. Because it's never been mine," Benji explained. "I wish my father and I could be closer, but I've resigned myself to that never happening. Really."

Dan smiled, "Don't worry, Ben. I don't want what you've clearly earned, but I'd still like to see where Ivan works."

Benji looked at his nephew and smiled. "Sure. Right this way." He stood and led them to the records room. He explained what everything was, what purpose it served, and how things were stored. He showed them Ivan's workspace.

Pete opened a desk drawer and picked up a framed, heavily degraded photo from the late 50s early 60s of a man, woman, and infant in a christening gown. "Who's this?" he asked.

Dan took the photo from him. "The man looks like... Geno Geneli, but given the age, I'd guess Salvatore."

"No, no. That's my Aunt Blythe. Ivan's the baby, and the man is Ivan's father, Andre Polaski. But...now you mention it..." Benji said, taking the photo. "I never knew my aunt or her husband. I never really looked at the photo before...just once when I was a kid before Salvatore Geneli moved to Chicago from Boston. Blythe was the black sheep of the family. Nanna didn't approve of Andre. I think this is the only picture of either of them. And Ivan always keeps it put away. It really does look like Salvatore." Benji looked up at Dan. "Why would that be?"

"Let's go find out, shall we?" Dan said, snapping a picture of it on his phone and putting the photo back in the drawer. He patted Benji on the shoulder and turned to leave, Pete and Gavin following.

At the elevator, before they parted ways, Pete leaned in and whispered, "So whatdaya think? Mr. Moore. Good guy or bad guy?"

Dan laughed, "It's too early to say definitively, but I'm

leaning toward good guy."

Gavin smiled. "His body language, tone, facial expressions…all read as genuine. He's either a sociopath or telling the truth."

"Gee. That's reassuring," Pete said. As the elevator arrived, Gavin and Dan stepped through the doors.

CHAPTER 62

"What can I do for you, Miranda?" Tom asked, not even bothering to look up from the box of "You're Never Alone" material he was searching through for some clue.

"Um. I had a dream."

He did look up at that, flabbergasted. "What?"

"I remembered something while I was dreaming. A speech Mike wrote but that he couldn't deliver because of his anxiety. So, I gave it. I got a copy of it out of MY boxes in the attic. See?" She stepped forward, pointing to the important part.

"It's a nice metaphor," Tom said, reading it.

"Yeah, I thought so, too. Except…"

"Except?" Tom asked.

"Mike was on the autism spectrum, Tom. He didn't use metaphors." Miranda explained, her voice cracking.

"Well. Damn," he responded, looking back at the quote. "Where's that box marked 'Wayne Carver'?"

He set the speech down and looked for the box among the stack of boxes Dan had brought down to him. He picked up his phone and called the Batavia police as he looked.

"Hey. Good afternoon. – This is Special Agent Tom Mathews. – Yeah. – Messenger over everything you have on a suicide in 2006. Wayne Carver. – Yep. – Of course, it's relevant." He hung up, finding the box.

He pulled off the lid. On top was a scrapbook. He flipped through the book. "Wow. How'd your brother get photos of evidence?"

"I...I didn't know he did. I have no idea."

CHAPTER 63

Salvatore Geneli sat across from Dan and Gavin. "What happened to you, Sergeant?" he asked, nodding at Gavin.

"Your son shot me," Gavin quipped. "Lousy shot, though. He mostly missed. I slammed into my car door, diving out of the way. Dislocated my shoulder."

"My sons are in this prison with me," Salvatore grinned.

"Not them, Andre. Ivan. Your other son."

Dan smiled wickedly. He had fallen prey to Gavin's inexplicable charm himself. Even if Salvatore was adversarial, Gavin would get him to talk. People wanted to tell Gavin everything. As much as he wanted to take the lead, he knew Gavin was better at this.

On his phone, Gavin pulled up an article from *The Boston Globe,* dated December 16, 1966. It gave details of an auto accident in which a couple, Andre Polaski and his wife Blythe, picked up a hitchhiker named Salvatore Geneli, a recent graduate of Boston University School of Architecture. Andre Polaski lost control of the vehicle and went over the side of a bridge. The hitchhiker was able to escape the vehicle unharmed, but Andre and his wife were both killed. They were survived by their ten-year-old son, Ivan, who was sent to live with his grandmother in Chicago after the accident. Gavin held it up so Salvatore could see it.

"Yes, I was in a car accident in 1966 before I moved to

Chicago. The driver and his wife were killed," the old man sneered.

Gavin flashed that smile...the one that charmed his victims...um...subjects, and opened his picture of Ivan's photo and held his phone up for the old man to see again. Salvatore, or Andre as it turned out, sighed heavily. "Idiot," he muttered. "I told him to get rid of that picture."

"So, you know everything then? I'm Andre Polaski. My wife's family didn't know what I looked like. I just changed identities with that hitchhiker. I looked enough like him. I followed my kid to Chicago. I found a better mark in Dominic Ricardi, so I just got Ivan to go along with the con. I planted him in Moore Industries when I figured out that Dominica had been having an affair with Ben Moore since she was 15 years old...just to cover my bases."

"Only he didn't tell you everything. Because he never told you about me. He's known about me for at least fifteen years," Dan taunted.

"What do you want from me? Sounds like you know everything there is to know," Andre said. Yeah, because you just told him, ya big moron, Dan thought. But Andre was obviously shaken by the news of Ivan's betrayal.

"I just wanted to see your face when you took that final fall from your high horse," Dan said, standing to leave. "Guard!" he called.

CHAPTER 64

Tom Mathews barged into Terrance Park's office, Sam Davis emerging from his own at the commotion. "You had evidence Wayne Carver was murdered, and you sat on it!" the agent bellowed.

Terrance rose from his seat behind his desk, staring at the FBI agent, unable to find any words to respond to the accusation. What could he say? It was true. He had sat on it. He'd been terrified for his own life, for his wife, for his daughters. But he'd never been satisfied that his fears justified his inaction.

Sam stepped forward. "What? What did you do, Terry?"

"Nothing!" he protested. Then he sat back down. "I did nothing." He buried his face in his hands. "I was afraid of Bowen. He personally killed that kid. He wasn't even afraid to do it. He forced the kid to write a suicide note, and then he hung him. A fourteen-year-old orphan. He scared the crap out of me! How…how'd you know?"

"Mike Davis copied everything you had. He put it all together. Figured it all out. And then he wrote a speech and dared Walter Bowen to do anything about it. Only his sister delivered the speech at the last minute. So, Walter didn't go after Mike. He went after Miranda. Or rather, he sent his sons after Miranda. One was the nice guy dating her roommate.

The other the monster."

"No!" said Sam, grabbing his chest as he collapsed to the floor. Tom rushed over.

"Quick, call 911!" he commanded, loosening Sam's tie. "Got any aspirin?" The assistant pulled open her drawer, pulling out a bottle of Bayer, and tossing it to Tom as she grabbed the receiver off the cradle and dialed 911.

Tom took an aspirin out of the bottle. "Water!" he called.

Terrance ran, disappeared into his office, and returned with a glass of water, taking it to Tom. Tom popped the aspirin into Sam's mouth and held the water to Sam's lips.

Tom glared at Terrance. "You're turning everything you have on Bowen over to the police. Today. Not that it matters. I already gave them Mike's copies. But you're cooperating thoroughly! You're resigning your partnership! You are no longer practicing law, Mr. Park, regardless of what the bar may do to you. Got it?"

Terrance nodded. "Yes. I got it."

"Walter Bowen's dead, anyway. I was just reading that his toxicology report shows he was poisoned," said the assistant.

"Where did you read that?" Tom asked.

"AP site," she replied.

Paramedics arrived, and Tom's attention returned fully to Sam. The new assistant called Connie.

CHAPTER 65

Deb returned to the Davis home, having spent the last two hours at the funeral home, going over details with the funeral director, reviewing her mother's obituary, deciding on a cemetery, and buying a grave plot. Fortunately, thanks to Dan's generous settlement, she'd been able to pay for it all. She punched in the code at the gate, Connie having given it to her that morning.

She'd left Jason in Miranda's care, not wanting to take a three-year-old to that type of meeting. To her surprise, Miranda was nowhere to be found. Neither was Connie. The house was oddly empty.

She found a note from Jameka on the kitchen table that Jason was with her and Angelica in the apartment.

She walked quickly across the patio and up the stairs to the apartment around the side of the garage. She knocked.

Angelica, wearing a paper feather headdress she'd obviously crafted with Jason, opened the door.

Jason popped up from behind a chair. "Mommy!" he whooped. "Angewica is hunting buffawo! I'm da buffawo!"

Angelica pulled off the headdress and smiled. "Yeah, I wasn't going to be the buffalo. No way, no how."

Deb burst out laughing. Jameka was sitting on the sofa, apparently also laughing at her mother and Jason's game but not participating.

"Where is everybody?" Deb asked, once she had hugged and kissed the "buffalo."

"Um. The hospital. Mr. Davis had a heart attack," Angelica said, putting back on the headdress and returning to her hunt. Jason was now hiding behind the kitchen island.

"What? Oh my God! Is he okay?"

"Yes," Jameka replied. "It wasn't a heart attack. It was angina, but they didn't know that when they left, just that he'd collapsed at his office. I hope it's okay that they left Jason with us."

Angelica snuck around the other side of the island and then jumped, pretending to shoot a bow and arrow, "Ah hah!" she exclaimed.

Jason giggled and pretended to fall over dead.

"Oh, of course! He seems to be enjoying himself," Deb laughed. "How'd you come up with this game?"

"That's my ma," Jameka smiled. "She was always making up fun games like this when I was little." Deb thought she was going to like Angelica Frost.

CHAPTER 66

Ben was trying to hold on. He was fighting the encroaching darkness, but he was finding it hard to concentrate.

Was Benji talking? No. That was Cameron, Benji's youngest boy. Where was Benji? Oh, there. Right by his side.

"Benji! Let's go to a baseball game tomorrow! Did you do your homework, Son? You know how your mother is."

"A baseball game sounds great, Dad. My homework's all done. Yes, I know how Mom is," his little boy said, taking his hand. "It's okay, Dad. I'm going to be okay."

What was Ben fighting against? What did he want to see? He couldn't remember. Benji. Something about Benji.

Oh, what difference did it make, anyway? Benji was okay. Benji was holding his hand. All was good. He closed his eyes and let it go, whatever it was. Sleep came. He was warm and comfortable. Little Benji, IV reached out to take his hand. "Come on, Grandpa. Your friend Dominica is waiting for you."

******

Benji sat silently, holding his father's hand until long after he felt the old man pass. He could swear he'd felt love coming from him for the first time in years. He wiped away a tear, leaned forward, kissing his father's forehead, and placing his father's hand on his now still chest.

"Goodbye, Dad. I love you. It really will be okay. You

left it all to a good man, anyway. I met him today. I like him."
Then he said to the spirit of his son, who had died when he
was 13 after being hit by a car. "Grandpa's with you now,
son."

He stood and left the hospital room, Cameron
following him out. Derrick, his oldest son, now 38, his wife,
and kids were waiting with Bridget, Benji's second ex-wife.
"He's gone."

"I wonder if we'll have jobs tomorrow," quipped
Derrick.

It was in the strangeness of the moment, of having felt
his father's spirit lovingly pass and being confronted by his
eldest son's anger and resentment, that he saw Dan Bradley
looking frazzled and anxious. He was at a near run, his friend
running behind him. He was looking for a room. That much
was obvious.

"Dan!" he called, waving his hand over his head.

Dan looked surprised to see him, but he strode over,
shaking Benji's hand for the second time that day. "Ben,
hello. Sorry. I'm looking for my fiancé. Her father collapsed
at work." He looked around nervously.

Gavin, likewise, shook Benji's hand, wincing a little as
his injured arm appeared to be bothering him.

"Oh, so you haven't come to claim your kingdom?"
scoffed Derrick.

"What?" asked Dan.

"My apologies. Derrick is upset. His grandfather just
passed," Benji offered, his tone suggesting Derrick zip it.

"Oh. Oh, I'm so sorry. Please, don't allow us to intrude.
We can transfer things when you've had a few days to mourn."

"Can't wait, Can you?" Derrick grumbled.

"Man, you don't know what you're talking about,"
Gavin interjected, stepping between Derrick and Dan. "He's

transferring it to your father, not taking it from him."

"My father left it all to you, Dan. You're within your rights to take it. It's what he wanted," Benji conceded.

Dan shook his head. "Only because he was deceived. Ivan Polaski planted a memo from you that proved to your father that you were part of the conspiracy to murder my mother and sister. Dominica changed her will before she died. She convinced your father to do the same. But they were wrong. Ivan and Walter were the real culprits. And then, after Kris killed Walter, Ivan and Kris started working together to just get revenge on us all."

"You expect me to believe you're taking nothing?" Derrick scoffed.

"Of course not. I'm taking my share. The exact same share you and Cameron get. I am cutting Kris out...if that's okay with you," Dan said, catching sight of Miranda. Relief washed over his face. "Excuse me. Miranda!" He ran to her.

Gavin scowled at Derrick and sauntered after his friend.

CHAPTER 67

Sam came home the next morning. Miranda stood on one side, Connie on the other, as he opened the front door.

"I'm not an invalid!" he argued for the billionth time on the trip from his hospital bed to his front door. He pushed his way through independently, despite their objections.

Ava and Tom Mathews seemed super cozy in the family room. Tom was still going through boxes, but he'd already uncovered Mike's case against Walter Bowen, as regarded to the murder of Wayne Carver. Tom, recently divorced, seemed to enjoy Ava's company. Sam moved on past them, heading through the butler's pantry.

Angelica and Jameka walked through the back door as Sam entered the kitchen. Hospital food sucked, and he was hungry.

"I'll cook you something, Sam! Please, just sit down," Connie pleaded, hurrying after him.

"Fine, but so help me God, Connie, if you try to feed me egg whites and plain toast, I'll throw it at you," he grumbled.

She rolled her eyes. "You haven't tried MY egg whites and toast," she pointed out. "And you'll damn well eat whatever the doctor tells you to eat, or I'll make your life hell. Do you understand me, Samuel Donald Davis?" Her eyes flashed, and she put her hand on her hip, tapping her toe. Well, she was awfully cute when she was mad.

"Retreat! Retreat!" Angelica joked to Jameka, drawing a smile out of Connie.

In the end, Connie made him a spinach Florentine omelet with Egg Beaters that was quite good, even though he wouldn't admit to actually liking it. He ate the whole thing, though, and his mood improved after he had done so.

Eventually, he settled in the living room, away from the crowd of people in their house but still central enough to feel a part of things. His doctor had prescribed rest for a couple of days, a heart-healthy diet, and an exercise regimen after he'd rested. He was also prescribed a beta blocker.

He was losing his mind, though. Everybody was tip-toeing around him, and it was irritating and way more stressful than had they treated him normally.

He watched his wife fussing over him, wishing she'd just relax. He changed the TV channel a few dozen times. The original black and white, "The Haunting," was on. He honestly hated the movie and book. It was something Mike and Connie shared. He, personally, didn't see the attraction.

He flipped the channel again. "Weekend at Bernie's." Now, this one he got. This one made him laugh. Mike had laughed, too, mostly because Sam laughed. Sam was never sure if Mike found the movie funny, another's laughter funny, or if he was just taking a cue from other people to laugh and not getting any of it.

In the end, it didn't matter. Sam had spent way too much time worrying about what Mike didn't "get." Right now, he'd give anything to have Mike watching this stupid movie and laughing…half a beat after Sam.

Connie brought him ice water and fluffed his pillow. Then she rearranged his throw.

"Jesus, Connie. I'm not dying. Stop fussing!"

"Okay. Okay," she responded, throwing up her hands.

She leaned over and kissed his nose before finally heading back to the kitchen. She bumped into the chess table on her way past. "Oops," she said, returning the pieces that toppled to upright positions. "Sorry, Honey." She turned and smiled at him, seeming completely unfazed by his mood.

The chess table didn't matter anymore. Nobody played anymore. He and Mike had played regularly. But neither Connie nor Miranda cared about chess.

And honestly, he hadn't cared all that much himself. He had only gotten the table because Mike had wanted to learn to play. He had taught Mike the game, and Mike had actually talked to him, somehow finding it easier to converse while concentrating on something else.

Over the years that they had played at that table, Sam had gotten to know the boy inside the tics and stimming. Mike was a complete person. It could be hard to understand that when he couldn't look you in the eyes and have a real conversation. But at that chess table, Sam had seen the complete person.

When he had been sixteen or seventeen, at that table, Mike had announced, "I want to fall in love. Like you."

"Is there a girl you like at school, Son?" Sam had asked, making a move.

"No. None of them are the right kind of person to love me." He had been matter of fact about it. No emotion was behind the declaration. It was just a fact. "A girl kissed me on the lips, though. It was an accident, but it still counts."

"How did she kiss you on accident?" Sam had laughed.

"She meant to kiss my cheek. But I moved."

"Ah." And Sam could swear he'd seen a gleam in his son's eyes…a mischievous look…like he'd moved on purpose.

"I want to fall in love with someone who can fall in love with me. The way Mom fell in love with you. She doesn't care that you aren't perfect. She loves you even when you are grumpy. None of the girls at school could love me when I am anxious or having a meltdown. Most can't even when I am calm because I am smarter than they are."

Sam had laughed. Mike's laugh followed half a beat behind.

Maybe the table did matter.

"Connie, I love you," he said. I'm sorry I'm a grump."

"I love you, too," she laughed.

"I'm going upstairs. You want me to rest? I'm going to rest. Okay?"

"Of course, Honey. Do you need help?"

He laughed. "No. I can walk upstairs by myself. I have my phone. If I need anything, I promise I'll call and ask for it. But tomorrow… all bets are off. Okay?"

"Okay. I accept those terms, Counselor," she smiled.

He turned off the television, grabbed his phone, and went upstairs.

CHAPTER 68

"Hey, Gabin!" Jason exclaimed, climbing on the sofa beside him. Gavin was leaning forward, and the boy climbed on his back, wrapping his little arms around his neck.

"I could have sworn I heard Jason's voice," Gavin teased, pretending to look around. He stood up, bringing the boy with him. "Where is he?" he asked, walking around the room.

Jason held on tight and giggled.

"Oh, there he is. I thought that was a mosquito!" He swung his good arm around, lowering the boy to the floor. "Hey, Jason. Good morning."

"Did you seep here wast night?"

"Yes. Is that okay with you? Or would you rather I not sleep here? Because I don't have to sleep here if you don't want me to," Gavin said, sitting back down and patting the sofa beside him.

"Oh, I don't mine. You could stay here all da time," the boy replied.

Deb, standing in the hallway, just out of view, had heard her son basically ask him to move into her house. He knew she had because he heard her gasp.

"Your mommy might not want that!" Gavin laughed, nodding toward the sound of Deb's gasp.

"Why not?" Jason asked.

"I...uh...I don't know. My staying here all the time is a big step. Besides, this house is more like your daddy's house than mine."

"What if we found a house together, then?" she asked, entering the room.

"What about...not ready for forever?" He grinned.

"Well, then you went and got hurt and proved me wrong."

He stood. He walked toward her. She backed up against the wall. He leaned in. She put her hand to his mouth.

"You'll catch me, right?" she asked.

He kissed her fingertips and took her hand into his. "You'll never hit the ground, Baby."

"How?" she sputtered.

"You talk in your sleep. By the way, I got to the bottom of that cliff because I fell first." He slipped the spider ring on her middle finger. "That kiss was something else."

"Ah. You still have it?"

Then he kissed her.

"Nana's brother says you are gonna get mawweed. So, you sould prolly stay with us all da time anyway," Jason said, playing with a dinosaur on the coffee table.

"Nana's brother? Who do you mean, Jason?" Deb asked.

"Mike."

She cocked her head. "Mike died, Honey."

"Yas, I knows."

"Well, if he died, how can he tell you anything?" she asked.

"I don't knows. He just tawks, and I hear him, just like you. Grandma told me it'z otay that I hears her and Mike. It'z not bad."

"No. It's not bad," Deb assured him. "But you can talk

to me, or Daddy, or Miranda, or Gavin…lots of people love you, Jason.

"Imaginary friend?" Gavin asked.

"Yeah. Yes. I guess. He's seen Mike's pictures and just given him a voice. He's been at the Davis house a lot lately."

"No. Mike's been my fwiend for a wong time. When da bad man took me, Mike told me I was going to be ok, dat Daddy and my Uncle Tom were coming to get me. He stayed wid me da whole time. He tawks funny, like a puter. And he rocks when he tawks."

CHAPTER 69

Dan opened the kitchen door. He found Connie apparently getting a cooking lesson from Angelica. Ava was assisting. Jameka and Miranda were sitting at the table, watching. He kind of stared, dumbfounded, as he closed the door behind him.

"What's going on?" he asked Miranda, who was watching from the kitchen table with a glass of wine in her hand.

"Mom said she needed to look up some heart-healthy recipes that Dad would actually eat. Angelica, it turns out, went to school to be a nutritionist when Jameka expressed an interest in pageants so they could both eat healthy and stay fit," she whispered as he sat next to her. "She offered to teach Mom a few recipes. Ava is trying to help."

"How's it going?"

"Oh great. Except Ava keeps wanting to add butter to everything."

He laughed in response.

"Butter tastes good!" Ava hooted.

"And clogs arteries!" countered Angelica.

"What are they making? It smells good," Dan interjected.

"Chicken Marsala," Miranda giggled.

"Without butter! That's a sin against humanity!" Dan

exclaimed.

"See?" Ava said.

"Trust me, will you?" Angelica said, spooning out some of the Marsala sauce for Connie to taste.

She tasted it and nodded. "It's delicious. But it's not Marsala," she laughed.

Angelica clicked her tongue. "You need to make some compromises."

"Where's Theo?" Dan asked, noticing one guest missing.

"Headache. She's upstairs," Jameka answered.

Tom came through the butler's pantry door into the kitchen, his face ashen.

"What is it?" Dan asked.

"Agent Belcher's body was just found in the private hangar at Dulles. He was strangled."

"Oh no! That's terrible," Connie said, frowning.

"It's way worse than that. Belcher's ticket was confirmed at the gate. According to American Airlines, he was on the flight to Chicago last night."

Over the next hour, a storm front rolled in. The sky darkened, and the wind picked up. By the time Gavin and Deb arrived with Jason, the rain was starting to fall. They ran from the Odyssey to the house. Lightning struck nearby, and the thunder cracked immediately after the flash. "Damn!" exclaimed Gavin, ushering Deb and Jason inside in front of him.

They found the household a bit somber. "Everything okay?" Gavin asked Dan as they walked to the family room.

"Not really. Agent Belcher was killed in DC last night. Kris apparently boarded the American flight using his ID and ticket. I'm just glad Jason is in the house now."

Gavin stopped walking. "He assumed Belcher's

identity?" Then, he shook off whatever thought had momentarily plagued him. "I've only got my service weapon on me. They took my spare the other night, and I haven't gotten it back yet."

"It's okay. Between the three of us, we've got it covered," Tom interjected.

The rain started pouring down as the storm increased in intensity. A large tree toppled across the street in front of the house in which Dan grew up. The lights in the neighborhood flickered and went out.

CHAPTER 70

"Dan?" Miranda said from the entrance hall, just outside the French doors. Her voice filled with fear.

Dan turned to the sound of her voice. Kris Bowen held her around her waist, his bowie knife held to her throat. Behind him, Ivan Polaski held a rifle pointed at them.

"Put your weapons on the floor and step back!" Ivan shouted.

They did as Ivan told them.

"Theodosia!" Kris called. "Theo? Baby? Where are you?"

Dan's heart sank. Damnit. He should have listened to Gavin. He'd never make that mistake again.

"Right here," Theo said, coming down the stairs.

"Why? You lost all claim to any money the second you started this insane plan," Tom said.

She smiled, all the sweetness and innocence she'd feigned gone. The Theo they thought they knew was replaced by an evil, calculating woman. "This wasn't for money. It was for fun," she scoffed. We sent all the money we need to live forever to the Dominican Republic before we killed Wally."

"Get the kid, Babe," Kris instructed her. His expression revealed his madness. "This is because you and this bitch think you deserve better than me."

"Kris, we never even gave you a second thought," Dan

said.

Kris twisted his features in anger. "Get the kid!"

Theo sashayed behind Kris. She seductively ran her hand across his shoulders.

"Of course, Darling. Be right back."

She pulled a second knife out of Kris's front jeans pocket, her hand lingering just a little too long. She winked at Dan. "That crazy old coot Frank taught me a few things. Like how to get in and out of places without people noticing. Of course, he thought he was helping to protect me." Then she turned on her heel, twirling the knife and opening it.

******

Deb had been a cop's wife, and when that marriage fell apart, she had been involved with a cop. And when he'd died, Gavin had become a part of her life. As a result, she'd become hyperaware. Plus she could swear she heard Gavin thinking at her to beware. Where the other women were busy and not paying attention to the muffled noises from the other room, Deb stealthily moved through the living room and peered into the entry. Gavin made eye contact with her. He barely moved his head, but she got the message. As quietly as she had snuck behind the trio, she hurried back to the kitchen. She grabbed the chicken Marsala pan off the stove, putting her finger to her lips, telling the others to be quiet. She pointed to the butcher block knife set. Connie grabbed a large knife. Deb nodded to the butler pantry door. Connie took a position against the wall by the door. Deb took the hot pan of food and did the same by the living room egress to the kitchen.

When Theo came into the kitchen through the living room, Deb threw the Chicken Marsala in her face. Theo screamed in anguish as the Chicken Marsala burned her face and neck. She blindly struck out with the knife she'd taken from Kris, stabbing Deb in the thigh. Deb yelled in pain. She swung the hot skillet at Theo, who threw up her hands to block the blow. She fell to the ground. Deb swung again, knocking her out with this blow.

"Dayum!" Angelica said.

******

Ivan and Kris turned toward the battle sounds emanating from the kitchen. Gavin rushed Ivan, knocking him to the ground and pinning him, yelling, "Sukin syn!"

Miranda, when Kris's grip loosened as he turned toward the commotion, twisted enough to bite his hand holding the knife. He screamed, dropping the blade. Dan grabbed her, pulling her free. Kris grabbed the knife off the floor and lurched toward Dan, brandishing the knife to stab him. A shot rang out. Kris Bowen fell to the floor, dead. Sam Davis stood at the top of the stairs, his weapon drawn and aimed at the spot where Kris had been. It all happened in a flash, but Gavin saw it all in slow motion.

"Deb!" Gavin called. When there was no answer, he yelled her name again. "Deb!"

He felt the panic start to rise when she called back. "I'm okay."

"Jesus, no, she's not!" yelled Ava. "She's got a knife stuck in her leg!"

Gavin scrambled to his feet, ignoring Ivan, who Tom promptly grabbed by the lapel and pulled to his feet, cuffing him. Gavin ran to Deb, who was sitting on the floor beside the unconscious Theo. "Oh God!" he yelled.

"It's not that bad," Deb replied, calmly.

"I think she's in shock," Connie exclaimed, rushing forward with several tea towels. "Do we pull it out?"

He looked at the wound as Dan, Miranda, Sam, and Tom, pushing Ivan in front of him, rushed into the living room.

"Uh, no. That will exasperate the bleeding. We let the doctors do that." He pulled off his arm immobilizer, lifted her, and carried her to Dan's cruiser parked in the driveway. He put her in the backseat. "Put pressure on the wound around the knife, Sweetheart," he said, packing the wound with the tea towels. Dan handed him the keys, as he called in the whole crazy incident to the Sheriff. Gavin flipped on the lights and siren and flew out of the driveway at about 80 miles per hour.

At the hospital ER entrance, he slammed the vehicle into park at the door, jumped out, and lifted her again, carrying her quickly through the door, calling out for help. She wrapped her arms around his neck and lay her head on his shoulder. "I love you," she whispered as she passed out.

CHAPTER 71

Life gradually returned to normal over the next few days. Deb's knife wound was mostly soft tissue, though the knife chipped the bone. She received 24 stitches and was told to stay off it as much as possible. Deb and Katelynn buried their mother. Deb placed her house on the market, and she and Gavin started looking for a home to share. Miranda and Dan returned to their wedding plans. Tom packed up his command center and returned to the field office. He maintained contact with Ava Bradley, though, and he agreed to be her plus-one at the wedding. Sam started his exercise regimen and returned to take over the hole left by Terrance Park's resignation. Once Sam was back in the swing of things, he and Dan met with Benji and his sons, distributing the Moore Estate as it should have been all along. Pete was promoted to Vice President of Engineering. Connie continued to cook, learning new, creative ways to make heart-healthy taste good. Theo spent a few days in the hospital but was then transferred to federal custody. Ivan was uninjured. He was taken directly into custody. He was dismissed from Moore Robotics and received no retirement benefits.

The week before the wedding, Dan sat in the Davis home family room, smoking a cigar and drinking whiskey with his future father-in-law, Gavin Mahoney, and Pete Camacho.

Sam pulled the box marked "Ellen/Elaine Bradley" from behind the bar and pushed it toward Dan.

Dan looked at it and sighed. He pulled off the lid. A letter addressed to him was on top of the contents. He opened it and read.

> *July 27, 2009*
> *Dear Dan,*
>
> *I have found out a few things about your mother and sister's murders. I don't know how to explain it to you. This box contains everything you need to know. I think the evidence will explain it better than I can.*
>
> *The only thing you need to know is I was curious because I caught a man stealing some videos off our security system. When I checked the files he copied, I saw something.*
>
> *Anyway, you want to be a policeman. I know you can make sense of all this.*
>
> *Your friend,*
> *Mike*

Dan looked at the evidence. It contained his mother's adoption records. It had been handled by Martin Feldman. Miranda had said Mike told her Martin Feldman had experience with adoptions. He had the memo from Geneli to Bowen Tobacco, agreeing to the hit. He had pictures of the Quincys and the Contis. He had everything. Years before the jewelry boxes even came into play. There was also a picture of the house in Sterling where Ellen and Carrie had died. A kid on a bike was riding a wheely on the street in front of it. Mike had labeled it "the neighbor boy." Dan laughed.

"What?" asked Gavin, taking a puff on his cigar.

"It just occurs to me. I've always thought I was Sherlock Holmes. Turns out: I'm Watson. First, with Mike. Now with you."

Gavin smiled. "Here's a question: why did Mike give those DVDs to Mary Cummings instead of just leaving them in the box?"

Dan shrugged. "Who knows? Why'd he put it in a box instead of telling the police? Maybe he realized they had killed him through Jane. And he wanted to separate some of the evidence. Maybe he just liked her and wanted to include her in his big secret. We'll probably never know. I talked to Manny Juarez. The missing woman he told us about that first night in Colonial Beach. It was Mary Cummings. They found her body in a dumpster on Monroe Bay a few days after we left. Kris and Theo searched her house for the DVDs, but she'd already mailed them to Connie."

He put the lid back on the box and shoved it to the side. "I bought the house in Colonial Beach. A wedding present for Miranda. Is that weird?"

Gavin burst out laughing. "Yeah, Man. A little. But it's a nice house. If it hadn't been for all the murder and mayhem, it would have been a fun vacation."

"What was that you said when you tackled Ivan, by the way?" Dan asked.

"I don't know. What did I say?"

"Suckin' sin?"

Gavin burst out laughing. "Sukin syn," he corrected. "It's 'son of a bitch' in Russian."

"Ah, money well spent. You minored in Russian at NIU, so now you can cuss out criminals in a language they can't understand," Sam said, rolling his eyes.

"How'd you know he minored in Russian?" Dan asked.

"Sam's known me since I was a kid, Dan," Gavin

reminded him.

"Oh, yeah. That's right. You're rich, and he's your lawyer," Dan teased.

"You're rich, and he's *your* lawyer, too."

CHAPTER 72

Dan and Miranda exchanged their wedding vows on a beautiful, sunny June afternoon at the country club, as Sam had always envisioned. The wedding ceremony was on the 18ᵗʰ green. Gavin was Dan's best man. Pete and Deputy Foley were groomsmen, which meant Gavin walked down the aisle with Camille and Deb with Pete, leaving Sally with Deputy Foley. Annalise, as a flower girl, followed Liam and Jason as ring bearers. Sam walked Miranda down the aisle to Dan.

The reception that followed the wedding was a true celebration.

Deb, unable to dance due to her injury, sat quietly, watching Dan and Miranda dance together. She saw Gavin across the room greeting an older couple. Wait...did the woman just grab his face and pinch his cheeks? She watched him laugh and sit with them. He seemed breezy. He never seemed breezy. Then he was making his way to her. He was smiling. God, that smile! Her insides did a flipflop. How did the mere sight of him manage to take her breath away?

Gavin sat down beside her. "Hey there. Why aren't you dancing?" she asked.

"Um, yeah. No," he laughed. "I'd rather sit here with you."

"Yeah, sure, sure. I get it. I'm amazing," she teased.

"You are," he agreed.

"I saw you talking to some other people. Are you coming out of your shell, Master Sergeant?"

"Me? God, no. They're my grandparents," he replied. "Wanna meet them?"

She turned and looked at him, stunned. "What? Today?"

"Yes," Gavin replied, taking her hand and pulling her up with him.

"Wait," she said as he led her away from the wedding party table and toward his grandparents' table.

"For what?" he asked, smiling. "They're here; you're here. They want to meet you." He was pulling her with him as he spoke. "Abuelo, Abuela, this is DeBella. Deb, my grandparents, Enrique and Lucia Fuentes." And she was suddenly standing at their table. He pulled a chair out for her to sit and another to put her leg up. She sat and shook both their hands.

******

Meanwhile, Sam looked at his plate of chicken and brown rice. Then he looked at the waitress's tray carrying a plate of the prime rib. He groaned. His wife patted his hand and kissed him.

Dan and Miranda wanted Mike's presence at their wedding, so there was a gorgeous memory wall set up with Mike's portrait and a running video on a screen with pictures of the three of them growing up together. Sam glanced over at it from his seat.

"I heard him, you know?" he said to his wife.

"What, Dear?" she asked.

"That day. When Kris...I heard Mike. I was asleep. And I heard him say, 'Wake up, Dad. Miranda needs you.'" He teared up at the memory. "I woke up and heard the commotion. I grabbed my gun from the gun safe...and..."

She touched his hand again and smiled.

"I heard him, Connie. It wasn't a dream."

"I believe you," she whispered, kissing him again.

******

Dan took Miranda into his arms and held her close. He wasn't much of a dancer, but he didn't care. She was his... all his...for forever. The DJ played "Kiss Me." Good idea, he thought. He kissed her. And the rest of the world sort of faded into a haze. It was just them, the music, and the dance floor. He heard Mike whisper, "About time."

Lacynda Mathes is a graduate of Radford University in Radford, VA. She holds a B.A. in English.

She is originally from Oak Grove, VA, in Westmoreland County near Colonial Beach. She graduated from Washington and Lee High School, Montross, VA, in 1986. She attended Randolph-Macon College, studied abroad at Wroxton College in Oxfordshire, England, and ultimately transferred to Radford University, where she completed her degree.

She currently resides in Sterling, IL, with her husband. She is the mother to their teenage sons, the eldest with special needs, who has been diagnosed with Lennox Gestaut Syndrome, a catastrophic childhood epilepsy, and severe autism.

www.ingramcontent.com/pod-product-compliance
Lightning Source LLC
Chambersburg PA
CBHW050727180626
46814CB00002B/633